The
Leaving
Summer

The
Leaving
Summer

DONAL HARDING

AN AVON CAMELOT BOOK

AVON BOOKS, INC.
1350 Avenue of the Americas
New York, New York 10019

First Avon Camelot Printing: June 1998

Printed in the U.S.A.

OPM 10 9 8 7 6 5 4 3 2 1

For
my mother
and in memory of
my aunt Wessie Rogers

—Acknowledgments—

Madison Smartt Bell; Jerry Cleaver; Rob Fromberg, at Northwestern University; Meredith Martin; Warren Scheideman, at DePaul University; and Shirley White supported and guided the shaping of this fiction. To them I shall be forever thankful; and finally, I doff my cap to all the Southern ghosts who seemed to know just when they were needed and appeared right on cue.

The
Leaving
Summer

—Chapter One—

$\mathcal{A}$tlas shifted his shoulders to get a better grip on the world. At least that's what Miss Dixie, our housekeeper, said happened in the summer of 1958. She said everybody in western North Carolina had to struggle to keep from toppling over.

Miss Dixie called me Mister. My name is actually Austin Carroll. If she was right and the earth did tremble under her bedroom slippers, it must have all started the week before my eleventh birthday. That's when Daddy brought the convicts home.

Daddy's blue pickup stopped at the edge of the backyard. Miss Dixie raised more than a little ruckus about the arrangement. "Oh, he done it now. When your mama hears 'bout this, there's more than tomatoes gonna get picked," she said, pausing to wrestle a pair of overalls through the wringers of the washing machine. "Convicts"—she adjusted the yellow scarf tied loosely over her hair and motioned with her head to the open basement door—"should be getting their comeuppance on the chain gang where they belong, not out there acting like free birds. When your mama gets back from Winston-Salem, she's gonna have plenty to say. This is just asking for trouble."

I pushed out the metal shutter to get a full view of Daddy's truck. One blond man tumbled from the front seat of the pickup, a second, older-looking one jumped from the flatbed. Dressed in blue, both stood, eyes downcast, waiting. Daddy came round from the driver's side, dropped the tailgate, and began hoisting bushel baskets into the arms of the men. The woven containers towered over their heads, forcing them to peek round the sides to avoid stumbling into a tree or bush. The window was near the corner of the house, allowing me to follow their movements. Daddy and the two men, stepping on one another's shadows, crossed the backyard behind our white clapboard house and walked into the sprawling tomato patch.

"Do you think they're murderers, Miss Dixie?"

"You stay away, whatever they've done." She came to the window, holding her wet hands high in the air so she wouldn't drop water on her dress.

"Daddy said they're trusty. They just look like field hands to me."

Miss Dixie frowned. "Well, Mister, they wouldn't be in

jail if they didn't go against the law." Miss Dixie noticed the tattoos on the arm of the older convict and pointed to him. "Men with tattoos are dangerous. Your daddy better get that one back to jail before nightfall." The steam from the wash water saturated the basement, adding to the sultriness of the morning. I began to taste the coppery minerals evaporating in my own sweat.

About the time the washing machine began to dance around and slosh water over its round belly, the basement filled with the smell of lilies and lilacs. Aunt Ada's perfume always arrived before she did. Miss Dixie said it was like a fog. I rushed out the door to greet Aunt Ada, who was our only true neighbor and one of my favorite people. She lived across the summer vegetable garden and through a dense patch of woods. Daddy called her an adventurer because she was the only person he ever knew who had been to Japan.

"Miss Dixie, you about finished with the washing?" Aunt Ada asked. Impatiently, she clicked a collapsible fan open and shut and stirred a lily-scented breeze, chasing away the musty smell of the dug-out basement.

"With all the commotion going on round here, I forgot I promised to help you sew. I'll be able to help cut out your dress in a jiffy." Miss Dixie ran a finger under the yellow scarf and scratched her head before dumping the wet clothes into the final rinse water.

"Well, you know I need a new dress for the Hendersonville dance," Aunt Ada said, smiling at me. She had promised to take me to the street dance with her, and I was looking forward to going.

I scooted back into the basement. Aunt Ada propped herself against the door. She flicked open the fan and raised it to shield her eyes. Peering into the tomato field, she asked, "Who are those men?" Squinting and moving her head forward like a chicken stretching for a lost grain of corn, she said, "One of them has snake tattoos on his arms."

"Both of them are jailbirds," I said.

"Mister-Mister, you hush up and get out of here." Miss Dixie pointed a finger toward the door and flung a few drops of wash water on my head. "Don't you be going down to that tomato patch." To Aunt Ada, she said, "The one that has marked himself up scares me. I tremble every time Mr. Carroll brings help out here."

Aunt Ada leaned to one side so I could squeeze by her. She whispered, "Better watch out or Miss Dixie will eat you alive."

I leaped from the basement door and ran to the dog-wood tree, jumping into the tractor tire strung with rope to the strongest limb. My bare feet stung from the short run over scorching grass to the swing. I stuck them straight out and tried to cool them down. I imagined a fire raging beneath the thin layer of topsoil. The heat hung so heavy in the air that birds rested silently on their perches and tomatoes puckered in the hostile sun.

Climbing the back steps onto the open porch that led to a smaller, screened porch, Miss Dixie explained to Aunt Ada that the sheriff let Daddy have the convicts to harvest the tomatoes. "When your sister gets home, there's gonna be plenty explaining to do," Miss Dixie said.

Aunt Ada lingered on the last porch step and exercised a practiced hand on her fan. Staring at the shiny bare back of the blond man, she said, "Convicts right here in Morningside."

Aunt Ada seemed as curious about the convicts as I was. I understood her curiosity. Miss Dixie said I had inherited the same flaw. She declared that Aunt Ada and I had to know the details of all happenings, whether they actually took place or we just imagined they might. I tried to break myself of the habit, but it was useless. The more I learned, the more I had to know. And outside of school and books, most of what I knew I learned from Aunt Ada.

I swung higher and higher to create a stronger breeze. The tomato patch fanned out below me, and I could see Shadow, our black-and-white spitz, standing guard at the edge of the garden, her tongue lolling out the side of her mouth. I could also see Grandpa's house, perched on the hill parallel to the one on which we lived. He had been born in the farmhouse and raised his three daughters in it. When he died, the hundred acres of farming land was divided among the three children. Four years had passed since my mother, along with Aunt Ada and Aunt Marble, who lived in Winston-Salem, inherited the land.

Aunt Marble did not want the hill country, as she called it, and immediately sold her inheritance to Mr. Hitcher. He and his two boys built a house so close to our property that Daddy said the rain off Hitcher's garage dropped onto our land. Mama said she was glad the Hitcher house was to the far side of Daddy's land. Even in winter with the stripped trees, a heavy growth of pines divided the properties and shielded our view. Daddy, who never spoke evil of anyone, warned me and Mama to keep our distance from the Hitchers.

Out of the corner of my eye I glimpsed the convicts hunkered down in the tomato rows. I wondered if I could get close to them without getting yelled at by Daddy or Miss Dixie. Daddy was grading tomatoes at the far end of the patch, and Miss Dixie was probably fitting Aunt Ada's dress. I left the swing, knowing this might be my only chance to get a better view of the convicts.

The tattooed convict leaned over a vine in the middle of the patch. The blond man was in the upper part of the garden, near the backyard. I walked toward him, keeping an eye on Daddy. If Daddy stood up or looked my way, I could run back to the swing.

Until a full-grown duck waddled out of the woods, the blond man appeared so concerned with picking tomatoes I thought he had not seen me approaching him. A baby chicken chirped at the duck's side. The convict said, "Well, look at that crazy duck. Don't even know its own kind." He fell back on the ground and wrapped his arms round his drawn-up legs. Sweat lined his face, and his arms and chest were wet.

"The mama hen disappeared. Daddy thinks a fox got it," I said. The man smiled at me. His gray eyes squinted against the glowing sun.

I moved closer, but stopped when the convict reached into the pocket of his blue work pants. I was scared he might draw out a knife, but out came two pieces of chewing gum, Teaberry chewing gum. His flat hand offered one piece to me. "Thank you," I said, taking the gum and shoving it in my pocket.

The convict snaked the other piece of Teaberry into his mouth, neatly folding the pink wrapper and pitching it into the high weeds outside the garden. Chomping, he looked at the hills surrounding us. My mouth watered from the sweet smell of the gum. "Beautiful here," he said. I looked up at uneven peaks. The green bushes and black shadows cast by tall pines failed to fascinate me.

I was trying to put together a question about being in jail when Daddy yelled, "Austin!"

I jumped to attention, and the convict fell back to gathering tomatoes. "What, Daddy?" I yelled back.

"Son, I've gotta go down to the store to get more baskets. You give the boys some water." Daddy wiped his forehead on his shirtsleeve. "Sure is hot enough out here."

"Yes sir, I will," I said. Then I was scared and ran to Daddy. "I'm afraid to stay here alone with them."

Daddy ruffled my hair. "Miss Dixie and your aunt Ada are in the house." He lifted his cap and looked at the men, who busied themselves in earnest work. "The sheriff wouldn't have let them out if they were risky. You know we've had workers out here before. I'll be back before you know it," he said, climbing into the truck.

All the while Daddy was preparing to leave, I was trying to figure a way to get water to the tattooed convict without having to go near him. The blond man seemed friendly, but like Miss Dixie, I suspected the other one might be dangerous. By the time Daddy started the truck, I had decided to fill jars with water, set them on the open porch, latch the screen door, and holler for the convicts.

After Daddy drove away I mounted the porch steps. The convicts stopped working and stared up at me. Selecting a mason jar from the small porch, I carried it into the kitchen. Miss Dixie and Aunt Ada jabbered in the back room.

Just as water shot into the jar, a darkness thick as thunderclouds covered the kitchen. I jerked from the sink. The tattooed convict stood at the threshold of the screened porch, mopping his wide brow with a yellowed rag. My hands started to shake. "I'm getting water for you. Just wait out there."

My fast prayer that he would stop outside the door went unanswered. The giant hand pushed open the screen door. Shadow edged in quietly beside him. The convict stopped with one tattered boot inside the door, waiting in that position, with Shadow's head resting on his advanced foot, while I drew the water. It seemed the jar had no bottom. I kept pulling away from the sink to check on the convict. He studied the tiny back porch: clay flowerpots of all sizes dripping pink, white, and purple blooms; mops; brooms; empty garden baskets; empty mason jars; and Daddy's Sunday shoes—all reflected in his eyes, eyes as quick as a spider's and as shiny as Daddy's shoes.

Miss Dixie was right; Mama would have a fit when she found out Daddy had brought convicts to Morningside, and one had been on her back porch.

Water sloshed from the overfull jar onto the floor. By the time I reached the back door, my feet were slippery wet. I shoved the water jar into the convict's hand. He stared at Shadow.

"That your dog, boy?" he asked.

His deep voice surprised me. I backed from the door and nodded. "Don't care much for dogs," he said, gently wagging his foot back and forth, shaking Shadow off his boot. His eyes shone like black marbles.

He drank the water so fast, he seemed to drain the jar in one gulp. A ring of water covered his heavy lips and made them sparkle. Returning the empty container, he backed off the porch. He stopped at the edge of the garden to ask, "Where is we?"

I pushed the screen door open and held it with my foot. "We are exactly twelve miles from Asheville and just 'bout the same distance from Canton. Canton's that way." I pointed west. He moved his head like he was drawing an invisible map. Shadow and I watched him shuffle back into the field.

I filled a second jar with water, leaving it in the sink while I hurried to my bedroom. The shiny cherry-wood box I pulled from under my bed had hinged brass handles on each side and brass straps over the top. A small lock that I never closed held a tiny metal flap in place. Aunt Ada had given me the box the summer before, saying I should keep treasures in it. "Commemorations for rainy days" were her exact words, and so it became my rainy-day box. I removed the lock and opened the lid wide enough to slip in the stick of Teaberry gum. Then I hurried back to the kitchen.

With the second jar of water carefully placed at the porch's edge, I ran to the swing. Standing on tiptoe, with the tire swing as far back as I could manage, I pushed off and glided over the open field. Suddenly, I plowed my feet into the spot under the swing worn bare by previous push-offs and stops, and the swing gouged into my back. My eyes scanned the tomato field and the small forest at the end of the garden. I surveyed every straight row drawn between the low, leafy plants, following the plow line at the edge of the plantings that divided the backyard from the woods. My heart pounded. My eyes fogged over. I tried to yell, but it felt like invisible hands were pressing all the air out of my lungs. The convicts had disappeared.

—Chapter Two—

I surprised myself by how calmly I sauntered into the room where Miss Dixie and Aunt Ada leaned over, pinning a paper pattern to red fabric. "They're gone," I announced from the doorway.

Bracing a mouthful of pins, Aunt Ada muttered, "Who's gone?" Tiny pearls of sweat decorated her cheeks. She stood up straight, pressing her hands into her back and arching her stomach forward.

"The convicts."

"Your daddy finally came to his sense and took 'em back to jail," Miss Dixie said, not even looking up.

"No, Daddy went for baskets. The convicts ran away."

Miss Dixie slowly lifted her head to look at me. She must have read truth in my face because she threw the red fabric on the bed, spilling a pair of scissors off her lap. "Lord have mercy." She squashed me against the doorjamb in her scramble out of the room. "Lord have mercy," she repeated, breathing hard and hurrying down the hall. When I caught up with her, she was in Daddy's closet, his shotgun flung over her arm and her hand blindly searching the top shelf for shells. "Go lock the front door," she yelled over her shoulder. Aunt Ada stood behind me, holding the retrieved scissors like a saber.

Aunt Ada and I locked the door and were heading to the kitchen when Miss Dixie yelled from the back porch, "Mr. Carroll's shoes are gone; his Sunday shoes I just polished. They're gone." Her shrill voice echoed through the house.

Aunt Ada and I looked at each other, but stood still until Aunt Ada whispered, "Let's go be with Miss Dixie. We need to stay together during this crisis." *Crisis.* I had not heard that word used before. There had never been a crisis in our house, in Morningside.

"That man would trust the devil. He is gonna be the death of us yet," Miss Dixie said. The three of us huddled round the kitchen table, waiting for Daddy.

"Why do you say that?" I asked.

"She just means your daddy's too trusting," Aunt Ada answered.

"And keeps everything to himself." Miss Dixie sat forward in her chair and leaned on the gun she held upright.

"The trusting taciturn," I said. I made a game of finding words that matched people; *taciturn* was my word for Daddy.

"You'd better hush them nasty words before they become habit," Miss Dixie said.

"*Taciturn* is in the dictionary," I shot back.

Miss Dixie raised one eyebrow and delivered her stare to me. "Just because some book got a word in it, don't mean you got to put that word in your mouth."

"Austin just means his daddy is quiet. And I believe he's a good man, Miss Dixie," Aunt Ada said.

"I know he is honest and true. He just don't talk. If he'd speak up and say something, his wife would be here and not in Winston-Salem."

I was about to ask what Miss Dixie meant when we heard Daddy's truck pull into the driveway, and my thoughts got lost in the commotion. Miss Dixie, hugging the shotgun to her chest, ran to the door. She flung the screen door back and yelled, "Mr. Carroll, them convicts you carried out here done run off."

Without a word, Daddy jumped back into the pickup and sped off. It seemed like forever before Daddy returned with four men. They searched the woods and all round and through our house and Aunt Ada's house. When the sheriff arrived, Aunt Ada guided him to the woods where Daddy and the other men were searching, and I began to feel better.

I was standing at the screen door when Bell Hitcher, the oldest of the Hitcher boys, ran through the tomato patch and bounded onto our porch. He held a blue metal rifle in one hand. "Where'd they go?" he demanded.

I thought he meant Daddy, so I said, "Daddy and the sheriff's men went down by the creek."

A belligerent glaze grew in Bell Hitcher's dirty eyes. "You idiot. I want to know where the *convicts* went."

I hunched up my shoulders. It was getting dark fast; all I could make out was the mean outline of Bell's face. He stomped his foot hard and swung his body from side to side. "You ain't nothing but a baby, a little baby boy." Aunt Ada stepped behind me and rested her hands on my shoulders. When Bell saw her, he backed off the porch, accidently upsetting one of the rocking chairs.

Miss Dixie sent me to bed before Daddy got back from taking Aunt Ada to her house. From my bed I heard Miss Dixie settle in a kitchen chair and start reading from the old white Bible, the same one she held every night she had her prayer meeting with the Lord. I heard her reading out loud until the song of the crickets overpowered me and hummed me into soft sleep.

Skipping in and out of dreams about running and chasing and hide-and-seek, I awoke to muted voices. Miss Dixie and Daddy sounded miles away until Daddy said, "I should have known better than trust convicts." I was sitting up in bed by then and could clearly hear.

"Now don't go blaming yourself," Miss Dixie said. "They just did what was human. Nobody to blame."

Daddy's footsteps advanced down the hall from the kitchen and neared my room. I put my head back on the pillow and closed my eyes, knowing he would crack the door to my bedroom and look in on me. Instead, I heard the door close to his room, and the sound of bedsprings confirmed that Daddy had settled down for sleep. I slithered from under the covers to hush any sounds my own bed might make. Inching the bedroom door open, I watched Miss Dixie fold her hands and pray.

—Chapter Three—

 $\mathcal{B}$ y the following week the excitement had died down in Morningside. Daddy and the sheriff had repeatedly scouted the hills and concluded the two convicts were in Tennessee by then. Aunt Ada and I were still scared, but Miss Dixie was more upset that Daddy's shoes had disappeared with the convicts.

Early Friday morning, Aunt Ada arrived to help Miss Dixie can tomatoes. She carried an important-looking stick, which I assumed to be a weapon. I was perched on the porch steps, leaning forward with two fishing poles propped beside me. "Well, well, it's the birthday boy," Aunt Ada sang, dancing up the steps. When she reached the top step, she whirled around to face the tomato field. "No sign of those convicts, I hope?" she inquired in a very earnest manner.

"Daddy thinks they're long gone," I answered.

"Well, that's a relief. I was afraid the men round here would catch them. That wouldn't have done anybody any good," Aunt Ada said, tossing the stick over the porch floor. It gave a little thud when it hit the house. I was confused. I had thought everybody was hoping the convicts would be caught.

"What—," I started to inquire.

"Bet you're going fishing," Aunt Ada said, like she didn't hear me. She swung open the screen door and let it slap shut behind her. Inside the house, with her voice becoming distant, she said, "That's the best thing to be doing on a day like this." Then she and Miss Dixie started complaining about being in the kitchen on such a hot day.

"If your sister was here to help us, we'd have these things done in no time and be out of this house." Miss Dixie's voice was loud.

I scooted back to the door and leaned an ear against the mesh screen to hear Aunt Ada's response. "I hope she is feeling better. I'm afraid she's going to go off the deep end if she doesn't come round."

As my reason dissolved into anger, I got ready to burst into the kitchen and demand to know why Mama was not home yet and why the convicts should not be caught. I had my hand on the door pull when B.J., an older girl who lived down the road, called my name. I grabbed the makeshift fishing poles, with hooks made from discarded hairpins, and ran to meet her.

Like me, B.J. was an only child. She lived about two

miles on the other side of the stubby hill to the front of our house. Other than the one-child families we came from, B.J. and I had only fishing in common. She wore glasses, had red frizzy hair cut shorter than mine, and cursed. She was supposed to be in the eighth grade, but was in the seventh with me. The previous summer, I tried to help her improve her reading, but she was not interested and I had little patience. To stay fishing buddies, I decided to forget the tutoring.

"I found a damn turtle," B.J. said, holding it up in the air. "Taking it to school next week." I had not seen her since the convicts ran away, but I knew B.J.'s daddy had been one of the men out looking for them. I half-expected B.J. to start right in pestering me for details, and I was surprised and happy she had found something more important. "If a turtle bites you, it won't let go till it thunders," she said.

As B.J. and I left the backyard and walked to the edge of the tomato patch, I couldn't help but wonder about the convicts. Shadow wandered ahead, waiting for us to catch up when she roamed too far. Her stump of a tail beat faster and faster with every step we made toward her.

Halfway across the garden, I paused and stared at the spot where I had squatted down and talked to the convict. The blood seemed to thicken in my veins, and my eyes blurred from the sun. I wished he had not run away.

Beyond the field, the earth dipped, careening straight

down a clay-packed ravine jagged with rock chips. We dug our heels into the hard dirt of the path, worn slick from earlier trips, and slowly descended the hill. At the foot of the path, a creek gurgled into a small stream that eventually fed into the French Broad River. We fell beside the creek under a black walnut tree to escape the direct sun. A one-lane wooden bridge, overgrown with honeysuckle and morning glories, forded the waterway and created an entrance to Grandpa's place.

"There used to be a road leading to that bridge." I was lying on my stomach and pointing to weeds, wildflowers, and wandering bushes that grew at will.

"I know it. Your grandpa lived up that hill before he died," B.J. said, sprawled out beside me. Shadow rested in deeper shade.

B.J. jumped up. "Let's go look inside."

I shielded my eyes and looked at the house. Nobody had paid any attention to it since Grandpa died. It needed to be painted. Something warned me not to go into the house, but boredom—along with B.J.'s enthusiasm—drove me up the hill.

Once we reached the hilltop, Shadow, B.J., and I stood in a straight line facing the house. The fan-shaped leaves of blackjack trees shaded some of the blank windows. Sunlight played with the shards of glass clinging to the edges of ivy-draped wooden window frames. The noon sun cut my vision to a slit. Clear, wavy lines came from the ground, as if someone had left an empty pot on an open flame.

Shadow broke the line, strutted a few feet, and froze. I followed her point. In the dim light of an upstairs window, someone watched us. I squinted and made out the dark hair and face of the convict to whom I had given water.

Still staring at the window, I started backing up. When I found my voice, I said, "Let's go." B.J. objected, but I was already running down the weed-infested hill, away from the house and her protests. I knew we could not get back home without being spotted and easily overtaken by the tattooed convict. When B.J. caught up to me, I said as calmly as I could, "Why don't we go under the bridge? It will be cooler and Shadow can take her bath." To prevent an argument, I added, "We can look at the old house later."

The moment the three of us settled under cover, footsteps shuffled above, showering us with sand that sifted through the cracks in the rotted wood. I held Shadow to prevent her from running out and giving us away.

"What was that? You saw somebody, that's why we're under here," B.J. whispered after the footsteps had faded.

I thought about what Aunt Ada had said about no one benefiting if the people round here caught the convicts. I was not sure what she meant, but I trusted her. I knew I had to get home and tell Aunt Ada the convicts were in Grandpa's house, but, more immediately, I had to quiet B.J.

"I don't know what that was. Somebody just got lost off the main road, I guess." I tried to sound hopeful.

"I know about them convicts. That was them." B.J. tried to push me aside.

"There were two convicts; only one person crossed the bridge. It couldn't have been them," I said, hoping to hush B.J. I must have sounded sincere, because she stopped pushing me and stood still.

She seemed satisfied with my explanation, but a knot grew in my stomach. Where was the other convict? Were the two of them waiting in the bushes up the hill? Maybe the blond convict got to Tennessee like Daddy said. Maybe we had only the tattooed one to face. I decided we had to risk the climb back home before what little nerve I had died or B.J. got feisty again. I peeped over the bridge, holding on to the decaying footings. A yellow butterfly fluttered above a blue flower. I motioned to B.J. to go up the hill first. If we encountered the convict, I would push her into him and run for help; I kept this part of the plan to myself.

Shadow did not bark all the way up the hill, which boosted my confidence about making it home to Aunt Ada. With each foothold on the bank bringing me closer to home, I calmed down and began to feel like myself. B.J. cleared the top of the hill first and disappeared down the road, hightailing it home. I took a long breath and started running across the tomato field, yelling, "Aunt Ada!"

By the time I reached the porch Aunt Ada had come to the kitchen door, wiping her hands on a small towel. "They're still here." I was breathless.

"The convicts?" she asked.

"Down at Grandpa's." I sucked for air.

Aunt Ada stared off in the distance like she was pondering a difficult mathematical problem. She threw open the screen door, looped the hand towel over the arm of a porch rocker, and swooped up her stick. "Come on, Austin," she said urgently. At the edge of the porch, she turned toward the door and yelled, "Miss Dixie, I'll be right back. Lock the doors."

—Chapter Four—

$\mathcal{W}$e used Aunt Ada's phone—the only one in the family—
to call the sheriff. Then we raced back and were explaining
to Miss Dixie why she had to lock up when three cars from
the sheriff's office roared into the backyard. Aunt Ada ran
out on the porch and pointed the sheriff and his four
deputies toward Grandpa's house.

After a half hour of searching, the sheriff came through
the tomato patch into the backyard. Aunt Ada left the
porch and walked to meet him. I stayed on the porch but
could hear most of the conversation. The sheriff said,
"Sometimes kids let their imaginations get the best of
them." He winked at Aunt Ada.

One by one the deputies gave up the hunt and squatted
on the grass in the yard or leaned on police cars. They
shook their heads and threw me shy glances. A skinny man

chewed the end of a straw and stared at me. I frowned at him because I didn't think he and the other men had searched hard enough.

Aunt Ada and the sheriff walked toward the men. The sheriff said, "You ain't got a thing to worry over. I'm going to speak to Mr. Carroll. We'll get it under control." He ran the tip of his finger along the brim of his hat.

"Nothing to worry about," Aunt Ada said, coming toward me.

"Do you believe me?" I asked.

"Of course, but we have to trust the sheriff. He said not to worry. He'll take care of things with your daddy."

"Take care of what things?"

"Now, Austin. I guess they'll set some trap to catch the convicts. I don't have any details and can't tell you more than that." It sounded like something she made up to end my questions.

The excitement and worry over the convicts took away any thoughts of my birthday until a high cake, smothered in chocolate icing and sitting on the ledge by the sink, caught my eye. I counted the yellow candles; the wicks of the remaining candles poked out of a small box nearby. Miss Dixie had miscounted. I stuck an eleventh candle into the soft frosting and licked my fingers. Miss Dixie had a problem with numbers. She laid all the blame on the Negro school she had attended, but Daddy said some people just never learn to figure without a pencil. When Miss Dixie worked in Daddy's store, I usually accompanied her to help operate the adding machine or to do the occasional arithmetic in making change.

Daddy was late getting home, but when he arrived he was in good spirits. He did not mention the convicts or the sheriff through most of dinner. I began to wonder if the sheriff had talked to him, so finally I asked, "Did you see the sheriff today?"

"Sure did," he said, scooping up a heaping fork of mashed potatoes.

"I really did see the convicts. I mean, I saw one of them down at Grandpa's." I wanted Daddy to believe me.

"Now that they know you saw them, they're gone for sure." He wiped his mouth with a wide white napkin. "Get the birthday cake, Miss Dixie. It's high time we celebrated Austin turning eleven."

Aunt Ada, who had been unusually silent during dinner, said, "I brought you this from my trip to Holland." She pulled a bright green box from under her chair and put it in my lap.

"I still can't believe you went to Europe," Daddy said, lighting a cigarette.

"You know I'm working my way around the world, country by country."

"Well, Ada, you are American, and you should stay in the country where you belong."

Aunt Ada stared at Daddy, and held the stare while she creased her napkin into several folds and tucked it under the side of her plate. "Open the present, Austin," she said.

I pulled a stem of the bow, and the ribbon fell from the box and draped over my leg. With fingers curled under the tight edges of the lid, I pried the top off. I fumbled through tissue paper until my hand struck something hard. The box fell from my lap, but I managed to pull a pair of wooden shoes from it before it hit the floor. Setting the shoes on the table, I admired their creamy, spotless finish. They were smooth as Miss Dixie's red velvet hat, the one she saved for special occasions. I couldn't wait to try them on.

"In Holland, the farmers wear them for planting," Aunt Ada said, running her hand over the upturned toe.

Daddy reached over and picked up one of the shoes, bracing a cigarette between his lips. "Heard about wood shoes, but never saw one. These would last a man a lifetime."

"It's a great present, Aunt Ada, thank you." I leaned over and gave her a kiss, then put the shoes on the floor and slipped into them. The wood was hard against my feet and my heels slipped up and down, making the shoes bang on the floor and sound like hammers.

"Just what we need, more noise in this house," Miss Dixie muttered, carrying the cake to the table.

"Blow out the candles, Austin. But wish something special before you do," Aunt Ada said.

"I wish Mama would come home," I said out loud. One

stubborn candle stayed lit after I blew out the others. Miss Dixie looked across the table at Daddy, but no one said a word.

With the dishes washed and racked, Miss Dixie, Aunt Ada, and I gathered on the back porch. I sat on the edge of the gray floor, dangling my feet over the side. Shadow laid her head in my lap. Miss Dixie and Aunt Ada reclined in twin rocking chairs that creaked out a little song. The hills turned navy blue as the final flickers of daylight drowned in a fuchsia sky.

"It's getting dark. We'd better turn on the porch light," I said, because I didn't share Daddy's opinion that the convicts were gone, and my sight was failing in the growing night. I wanted to make sure the convicts didn't sneak up on us.

Miss Dixie said, "We can't put no light on, or we'll get eat up by the bugs." She slapped at a mosquito.

Daddy, who had disappeared right after supper, joined us and sat in the porch swing.

"Is everything all right?" Aunt Ada asked.

"Everything is all set," Daddy said.

I was ready to ask what was set when the bushes beyond the tomato field rustled. I scooted up from the porch's edge and embraced the post. "What was that?"

"Oh, just the fireflies," Miss Dixie said.

"Fireflies," I mouthed, turning to the three faces hidden on the darkened porch. "Fireflies?"

They were silent, except for the creaks, snaps, and

wheezes coming from their rocking chairs. Within a heart-
beat all sounds left the evening, even the chorus of crickets. Then the bushes ceased to move and crickets sang
again.

Suddenly, as if a giant firefly had exploded, the inked
sky ignited with crimson and orange flames. "Look at
Grandpa's," I shouted. "Grandpa's house is on fire." I turned
around to see three faces animated only by the raging scarlet blaze. Shadows played at their eyes. I expected everybody to be jumping up and running to the fire, but they
were immobile. "What's wrong? Aren't we gonna stop the
fire?" Grandpa's house became an orange square, with the
fire growing stronger, like a runner getting his second
wind.

"Son, we should have got rid of that house long ago,"
Daddy said in a low voice. "Empty buildings just cause
trouble. It's best to let the place burn up. A good burning is
the only way to start fresh, like when we burn off a crop to
clear the ground."

Miss Dixie sat at the edge of her chair. "Ain't you afraid
the fire will spread?"

Daddy shook his head. "The sheriff's men will check it.
No need to worry about the fire going beyond that old
house."

Aunt Ada released her chair. It rocked on without her.
At the edge of the porch she stopped and stared at the
burning house. The way she looked at the fire told me she

knew the house was going to burn before it even started. She knew. They all knew about the fire. It was planned. I had put all my trust in Aunt Ada; she was the one I ran to after I saw the convict. Aunt Ada had never kept anything from me before, but this time my trust in her went unreturned. She had kept the fire a secret.

Stepping off the porch, Aunt Ada lifted her shoulders, wrapped her arms around herself, and gazed at the fire. "Those flames are burning the past," she said.

To stop my hands from shaking I clamped them onto the swing's armrest and scooted close to Daddy. He rose, taking a last whiff from a cigarette. "Better let me walk with you, Ada."

"No," Aunt Ada replied. The way she said it sounded like she was still mad at Daddy for scolding her about traveling outside of America. She turned toward the road and ran into the darkness.

Daddy shrugged his shoulders and said, "Can't figure women. Sometimes they're afraid of a spider, other times they're not afraid to stand right up to the devil." Daddy ruffled my hair. Before he disappeared into the house, he paused and stared at the fire. "When you're a little older, things'll fall into place. You'll see." Daddy spoke as if my age held some grand patience that would eventually be rewarded. But when? Turning eleven years old had not made any difference.

Miss Dixie was at Daddy's heels. Pausing with her hand

on the doorknob, she said to me, "Mister, you'd better get in here. No telling what's out there in the dark."

"Just fireflies, Miss Dixie, that's all that's out there in the dark," I snapped.

She flashed her eyes at me, then disappeared inside. Her squishy footsteps faded down the hall.

I was ready to move toward the door when Daddy's voice stopped me. From the kitchen, but out of my view, he said, "We've got to go to town pretty soon and get you a new bicycle. It'll be your birthday present from me and your mama. You can pick it out."

"Okay, Daddy," I said, easing back down in the swing. I could not concentrate on presents with Grandpa's house burning to the ground.

Alone, I sat on the porch, watching flames spiral into an inverted cone. Irregular sparks danced to muffled blasts in the distance. Small terrors crept up my back. The hard slats of the swing drove away any desire for sleep. I sat strapped to fear and waited for the fire to exert its full violence.

In slow motion the brightness of the fire dimmed, faded, and lulled me to sleep. If I dreamed, I cannot recall, but I remember clearly the awakening.

I jumped as if someone had given me a punch. I struggled upright in the swing. A stream of gray smoke swept up from the charred foundation. A single chimney stood, a survivor in the early mist. Pink and blue morning glories opened with the dawn. Dew glistened on the grass and wet my hair. I stared at the thin line of smoke that had replaced

Grandpa's house. I was startled at finding myself outside, but more surprised that Miss Dixie had allowed me to stay out all night.

I had kinks in my neck from crunching in the swing. I pulled my head forward, then rotated it side to side. The movement swept away the grogginess of sleep and let my eyes concentrate on the porch. The fear from the previous night returned, and I closed my eyes to block out the terror. Slowly, I reopened them to stare directly at what had reawakened my fear.

With hands taut on the swing slats, I braced myself. My heart began to beat faster and still faster until the swing seemed to tremble under me. Daddy's Sunday shoes, the ones that had vanished with the convicts, sat at the edge of the porch.

— Chapter Five—

$\mathcal{M}$iss Dixie swung open the screen door, thumped across the floor, and kicked the returned shoes off the side of the porch. She dusted her hands up and down. "Fine morning, ain't it, Mister?" she said, surveying the mountains, which were gaining color from a growing sun.

"Where'd those shoes come from?" I demanded.

Before I could ask again, Miss Dixie stepped off the porch, bent over, and ran her hand across dewy clover. "Four leaves. Just saw it out the corner of my eye. Lucky day," she said.

"Miss Dixie"—I raised my voice—"who brought the shoes?"

She climbed back on the porch, twisting the clover leaf in her fingers. I watched the footprints she left in the wet grass. It seemed she would walk right into the house without a word to me, but suddenly and quietly she said,

"Somebody that don't need 'em no more."

"Are the convicts dead?"

Miss Dixie gripped the screen-door pull and glared at me like I had insulted her. "I'm gonna get your daddy to wear you out if you don't quit pestering me. Now, get in here and wash them hands for breakfast." She held the door wide open. When I was within her reach, she grabbed for my ear. "And you'd better shut up about things that need to rest." I pushed at her with my hip. Her generous hand slapped me on the fanny.

Just as I swallowed the last bite of egg, heavy footsteps clomped across the porch. For a moment I thought it might be the convicts returning. I watched the screen door. Bell Hitcher's trim figure appeared on the porch. He pressed his face into the mesh screen. Daddy got up and met him. Miss Dixie carried her plate to the sink, then turned to the stove and lifted the lid on some meat she was cooking.

"Don't mean to bother, but wanted to rest your mind about them convicts. As bad luck would have it, I only got one of 'em, and I'm not even sure he's dead. The other one got away. He can probably blend in as a hired hand somewhere, but I'll never give up looking for him."

I perked up and tried to listen over the clamor of the pots and pans Miss Dixie juggled on the stove. Bell jerked his hand up and down as if he were telling Daddy in sign language where this had happened.

Daddy looked over his shoulder at me and Miss Dixie.

I jumped around and pretended to be interested in Miss Dixie's cooking dilemma. Bell pulled open the screen door, and he and Daddy walked out of sight.

I guessed that Bell was pointing Daddy to Yankee Hill, the small, steep slope rising behind Aunt Ada's house that had a history going back further than anyone alive could accurately recall. Every time I questioned Daddy about the hill, he would look me straight in the eye and say there was nothing up there to be proud of. The hill got its name from a Yankee Civil War deserter buried under an aged, man-size stone. The story went that my Grandpa's mother was attacked by the deserter, but she fought and killed him. Afraid other soldiers might take revenge, the family secretly buried the deserter on the hilltop.

My curious nature had taken me to the top of that ridge several times, long before the convicts escaped. I knew my way around Yankee Hill, despite Mama's warnings of bears in the hills.

If Bell was right and one of the convicts got away, an escape through the mountains would not be easy. The perpetual blue haze hanging over the rugged, steep peaks made the higher ground almost impossible to manage without getting lost. Much of the mountain territory was so overgrown that some of the highest ridges were unexplored. A few houses dotted the area, but for the most part, trees, plants, animals, snakes, and Indian spirits were the only things living in the hills.

• • •

I was still seated at the table when Daddy returned to the kitchen. He paused beside me, reached for his coffee cup, and drained it. "Boy, Miss Dixie's coffee is real sour when it gets cold." Miss Dixie did not hear, because she was talking to herself and checking the pantry. "You get ready now, Miss Dixie. I'm going to drop you at the store," Daddy said louder, to get Miss Dixie's attention. He pulled on his cap and ruffled the back of my hair, the only attention he had given me all morning.

"What did Bell Hitcher want?" I asked.

Daddy's shoes creaked across the kitchen, but he closed the screen door so gently I thought he was sneaking out. I watched him pluck a Camel from his shirt pocket before he answered, "Nothing."

Miss Dixie tugged at her apron strings. When she worked the knot loose, she pulled the apron over her head and hung it on a long nail in the pantry. She stared in the little mirror over the sink and said, "I hate tending that old store. Sure will be glad when your mama gets back here." She started for the back door, then turned to me. "You be sure and get yourself down there to help me stock them shelves."

"I won't forget. I'll be there this afternoon." I chose my words carefully so as not to delay her.

I stayed on the porch until the truck backed onto the road that threaded the Hitchers, Aunt Ada, and us together. With Daddy and Miss Dixie out of the way, I planned to visit Aunt Ada and then to climb Yankee Hill. When the truck pulled away in a cloud of tan dust, I made a high dive off the porch, shot through the woods dividing us from Aunt Ada, and was catching my breath in her backyard before the pickup was out of earshot.

Aunt Ada's garage stood free of the house, and her car wasn't in it. I turned and looked through the thick treetops up the skinny hill that started at my toes. I would climb Yankee Hill and hope Aunt Ada had come home by the time I returned.

Shadow whined at my side. I stooped and patted her head. After a few deep breaths, I plowed into the cleared part of the woods, meeting thicker growth with each step. Shadow sat on her hind legs, watching me. "Come on, Shadow. We don't have all day." She crept to me, keeping her tail low, a signal that she objected to the climb up Yankee Hill. She came out of loyalty, not enthusiasm.

Briers and sticky leaves slowed our climb. When Shadow and I were halfway up the slope, I stopped to think about what I might find or what I should be looking for. Maybe I would find a shotgun casing for my rainy-day box. A morning bird sang, "Here she comes, here she comes." If I could have whistled like Daddy, I would have replied.

I cut a path through heavy underbrush thick with thorns, stopping every few steps to unhook my shirt or shorts from reaching limbs or snarling brier bushes. I circled a downed tree, avoiding forked branches jutting out from the trunk. Feeling safe from the tree's reach, I quickened my steps. Just as I did, a branch, sharp as a knife, stuck the rim of my ear. Blood spurted and ran down my neck. I plugged the cut with my finger. A thin line of blood ran down my arm, collected at my bent elbow, and dripped to the ground like single red raindrops. My ear was hot. I flinched at the raw pain. I held my head to one side to stop the bleeding, but a pool collected in my ear and made a seashell sound. I closed my eyes and shook my head, pelting Shadow with flying blood.

I was still petting my ear when I reached the hilltop. The terrain evened out, with white pines framing a neat clearing. When Shadow reached the crest, she broke and ran ahead, and a wide holly bush hid her from me. I threaded the shoulder of a gully bleached pale pink from summer sun. I slowed my steps to concentrate on the area. Sharp points of holly leaves glistened before me. For a moment the sky was empty, and then I saw a bird, probably the one singing to me on the trail. An occasional fly buzzed by, breaking the silence. Without another thought, I stepped clear of the holly branches and joined Shadow.

The old stone covering the Yankee soldier was planted deep and edged with standing weeds. Shadow stood beside the grave, her nose polished with red clay and her front paw trampling a daisy. Next to the familiar stone, weeds were twisted, bent, and caught in several mole holes; Shadow had rooted into one and tossed fresh earth around the rim of the hole.

I looked around, trying to figure out why Bell Hitcher had motioned toward the hill. Not finding any evidence of a struggle, I suspected Bell Hitcher had lied to Daddy. I started feeling unsteady. My forehead was damp, and I couldn't tell what was making me sweat, the direct sun in a cloudless sky or the discovery that the hill remained the same as on my previous visits. The trees seemed to wave around me. I squatted to catch my balance.

No more than ten yards from me, a blue rag lay caught under a dead limb; the convict's shirt, probably lost in his flight up the hill. I struggled to my feet. Shadow whined and jumped round in circles, and I stopped to quiet her. While bending over, I thought I caught a glimpse of something moving. It was a quick motion that I hoped was caused by a bird. Shadow's whines turned to growls. I jerked up, searching the trees and the hilltop; not even a butterfly to be seen. Nothing.

The smell of moss and wild grass filled my nostrils. Wiping the sweat of a full summer and spitting out a dog hair I had sucked into my mouth, I moved in slow motion toward the shirt.

Just as I reached the spot where the shirt lay, I heard a moan. I remembered Mama telling me that bears roamed the mountains. I knew also that this land once belonged to the Cherokee, and I believed their spirits still lived in the trees. Shadow barked loudly and backed up, turning in fast circles. Expecting to find either towering black fur or a war-painted Indian, I shifted my head and let my body follow. My foot tangled in ground vines, and I tumbled to the floor of the forest.

On this part of the hill the trees grew thickest, and their leaves blocked the direct sun. What little light filtered through the trees got caught in tall weeds and made strange green patterns on everything it touched. My hand, which had landed on the blue shirt, looked like it had been marked with a moving green tattoo. At first I thought my imagination was playing tricks on my eyes, but then I felt the shirt move under my fingers. I jerked back.

My eyes refused to close; they burned from lack of reprieve. My short breath heated my cheeks. When I allowed myself to focus, I realized the shirt had arms and a head; legs grew out of the bottom. I had found one of the convicts.

—Chapter Six—

$\mathcal{I}$t was the blond convict, and he lay belly-down with his arms stretched out on each side of him; the blue shirt was spread open. One pant leg, ripped to the thigh, revealed the back of his calf. Only part of his face was visible. I grabbed onto a pine trunk to right myself and steady my legs; the bark scraped my fingers.

Shadow kept barking, her gaze switching between me and the man. I had to think. "Shadow, shut up," I yelled. The volume of my own voice drove me flush against the rough tree trunk. I wished it would open up and take me in.

I let my body slide down the scratchy tree until my chin rested on my knees. Then I tipped over on my knees and crawled near the man. He might be playing possum, and if I got within his reach, he could grab me. I inched forward, straining to see his face. He had tunneled into a bed of dead leaves, with bushes pushing up around him and low tree branches swaying over him. Moss softened the ground under us. When I got close enough to see his face more clearly, I held back and watched. The bit of face I could see was caked with dirt and crumbled leaves. His eyes were not held by will; they were naturally closed, as if he was asleep. His breath spurted out like he had taken a hit in the stomach. A blue jay's feather clung to his parted lips; it fluttered when his breath crossed it. Convinced the man was knocked out, I sat back on bent knees and inhaled, then forced the air back out my nostrils, trying hard to exhale the balance of my fears. Never before had my heart pounded so, nor had my hands jumped from such fright.

Feeling braver, I leaned slightly forward. Before I could stop my hand, the blue-striped feather was in my shirt pocket, destined for the rainy-day box. The bird that called to me earlier was now perched somewhere above. It sang, "Here she comes, here she comes." My eyes left the ground and searched the poplars, oaks, and pines. When I looked back at the convict, his eyes were open, or at least the one I could see was. It was as reflective and cold as silver. Without moving his body and before I could react, he reached up, caught my shirt in his fingers, and downed me. We were face-to-face, and his sour breath echoed in and out of my open mouth.

Watching my reflection in the silver eye, I thought he might not recognize me, so I said, "Do you remember me? The chewing gum? The field?" His fingers kept me. I pulled my chest back, trying to get free. "Please," I said. His eye opened wide. My hands pushed at his fingers.

Just as quickly as his hand had seized me, it melted. It seemed he had used the last of his energy, and his eyes closed again. I rolled back on the moss and caught my breath. My heart pounded so hard I felt my chest move against my shirt. Shadow nudged her nose under my chin and whined until I pulled upright. The bird still sang somewhere above.

When my mind settled and my eyes could focus, I realized my hand remained on the convict's. I jerked it away. But then, without reason, I reached out and laid it back. My skinny fingers rested on width and length that were years away for me. I tried to control my shaking hand and hold it steady to let the touch of my palm bring comfort to the man.

Shadow held her tail still, staring at the tree where I had regained my will. I released the man's hand and rolled over to face what held Shadow's attention: the other convict braced against the side of the pine. One bare foot propped on top of the other. Seeing him surprised me, but what seemed unbelievable to me was that I wasn't afraid.

"I dragged him this far, all the way up that hill. But it ain't safe up here. A man with a gun circled up this way," the convict said, moving his head to one side and looking over his shoulder at the pines and bushes behind him.

"Will he live?" I asked.

"If he gets help and if that man with the gun don't catch

him." He wiped his face with his shirtsleeve. "I've done all I can do. Can't make it with him." The man straightened up and pushed against the tree.

"Where are you going?" I asked.

"That way to Canton, you said?"

"Yes, but it's hard to get over the mountain." I got up and walked near the man. When I was close, I could see one of his feet was bleeding just above the big toe. I kept looking at his toe, but pointed and said, "Go down that way. It's not so steep and there's a little path that leads all the way to Horn Gap. When you get to the end of the path, you'll be able to see Canton."

The man worked his foot over a lumpy tree root and stopped. I pulled back a little. Without a word he leaned toward me and stuck out his hand. With our hands still together we both glanced at the wounded convict.

"I'll take care of him," I said. The man studied his own feet, and I thought he might be wishing somebody could take care of him. I squeezed his giant hand as best I could. He hurried away in the direction I had pointed, and I returned to the downed convict.

I studied the man's back and wondered what to do with him. I could hide him in the old chicken house, turned over to me last winter after all the chickens disappeared. The only time it was ever used was at Christmas, when Daddy would keep the tree there until the sap healed at the cut. But moving the convict there had one serious drawback. Daddy kept his hunting dogs in a fenced pen a few feet from the chicken house. Any noise would have them barking their heads off.

I could not think of a safe place to hide him. I needed help. *Aunt Ada?* She might call the sheriff. *Miss Dixie?* She would panic and might even faint. *B.J.?* No. *Daddy?* He would not be home until sunset, and he would get the sheriff. Aunt Ada. I had no choice but to trust Aunt Ada.

— Chapter Seven —

By the time I reached Aunt Ada's front porch, I was ready to explode. I banged on the screen door, shouting, "Aunt Ada, help me." When she appeared, I blurted out, "I found one of the convicts. He's alive." I described the wounded man's condition and told her about giving directions to the second man, but mostly I begged her to help save the convict and not to call the sheriff.

I sat on the edge of the green rocker in Aunt Ada's living room while she doctored my ear. Something about her looked different, but I couldn't decide what it was. When I mentioned that Bell Hitcher had told Daddy he was after the convicts, Aunt Ada began to pace around the room. She halted in front of the fireplace. The mantel held Aunt Ada's collection of porcelain ladies in long skirts. She ran a finger around the blue parasol held by one of the figures. I sat still, waiting for her decision. Moving into the center of the room, Aunt Ada pivoted on her high heels as if she might sit down on the sofa. Instead, she circled her arms around her waist and drifted back across the hardwood floor. She floated around the room like a mimosa seed caught in a soft breeze. The only sound came from her clicking heels.

Aunt Ada stopped dead still. Her back was to me when she said, "Austin, this is a dangerous man. He was in jail. This is the sheriff's business." Aunt Ada's reaction showed me I had to try harder to convince her.

"But look what happened yesterday when you called the sheriff. Grandpa's house burned up, and I just know Bell Hitcher had something to do with it. And now if Bell finds this wounded man, I have a bad feeling he will kill him. I don't want to catch the convict, I want to help him." Aunt Ada faced the phone, her back still to me. "Please."

Aunt Ada turned to face me. I took this as a good sign. She said, "I'm afraid." I wondered if she was afraid for me or her or the convict.

"He's nearly dead. He can't hurt us. He didn't hurt me." My voice was flat. I could have been trying to convince myself. I said, "I just know he's not dangerous. You've always told me to find the child in people and they will be on my side. He needs somebody to help him. Aunt Ada, please, please help me." The words left bitter traces on my tongue. I hated begging, seldom resorted to it.

We left the house without another word spoken. I don't

know what I said to convince Aunt Ada or if she had her own reasons, but I suspect she could not pass an opportunity to atone for whatever part she might have had in the burning of Grandpa's house. Aunt Ada forgot to change her shoes but remembered to pick up the stick she wielded as a weapon.

I led the way up the trail, holding back branches that hung over the rugged path. The climb was slowed by Aunt Ada's high heels. After only a few steps up the hill, I stopped and looked back at her. "Aunt Ada, do you have a gun?" She raised her eyebrows, which I took to mean she didn't. "Oh. He's unconscious. I was just wondering."

The only sounds on the trail were murmuring trees. I wished for the songbird that had accompanied me earlier. Midway up the hill, Bell Hitcher jumped right in front of me. I stopped so quickly Aunt Ada fell against my back.

"Where you going?" Bell asked. A brown cap spotted with old sweat covered the top of his face. He planted the butt of his rifle beside him and propped himself on it.

Aunt Ada took hold of my shoulder and stepped in front of me. We both looked up at Bell's squared chin. "This is my land, so the question is, where are *you* going?" She planted her stick next to his gun and put her hands on her hips. I saw the tips of her fingers shaking, and that made me shake.

"Now, lady, this ain't no place for a woman and a boy." He pointed his head toward me. "Don't you know these woods is dangerous? Why, even a growed man could meet his end up here."

Aunt Ada stood up straight. Her shoulder blades rose and stood out like small angel wings.

"Well, I'm just shortcutting over to McCallisters'," Bell Hitcher said. I could tell Aunt Ada's pose made him ponder.

"Just because your father bought land that borders my land gives you no right to cross my property. Use the road to get where you need to go." Bell Hitcher reared back and crossed his arms. Aunt Ada dug her hands into her hips. "You are never to set foot on this land without an invitation. This is the way out." Aunt Ada pointed to the path we had just climbed.

Bell Hitcher drew in his shoulders, and his eyes bulged out like he was ready for a bloodletting. I thought he was going to slap Aunt Ada.

Aunt Ada's back stiffened. "Get off my property. *Right now.* And if I ever see you here again, I'll call the sheriff." I stood behind Aunt Ada, feeling the intensity of her command. Bell tucked his head, threw the rifle over his shoulder, and walked down the hill.

We waited several minutes until he disappeared and his footsteps died in the grass at the bottom of Yankee Hill. "Do you think he knows?" I whispered into Aunt Ada's ear. She put her finger over my lips.

My stomach was tied in knots by the time we reached the convict. To my surprise he was on his back, and his eyes were open. He stared up at us. A gaping wound ran down his left side, scarlet traces fading to brown covered his chest. Scuttling back as we approached, he winced in pain and dragged himself farther into the tunnel he had made.

Aunt Ada stood a good distance from the man. To show her she had nothing to fear, I moved closer to him. I could stand the silence no longer. Looking down at the man, I said, "We're going to help you." I fell on my knees, shrank my head into my neck, and hunched forward, resting on my hands. The convict's head rolled back and rested on soil still damp from morning dew. I thought he smiled. I forced my hand to his and held it flat.

Aunt Ada inched closer until finally she stood at my side. Bending over the convict, she reached out her hand, hesitated, and jerked the shirt over his wounds. She said, "We are going to help because we are good people." Her voice was firm but kind. I couldn't tell if the convict heard. Aunt Ada stood up straight again, looking around the hill and seeing what I had seen earlier. I was still squatting on the ground. She said, "Bell Hitcher might see if we move him in daylight. We will have to come back when it's dark. Let's drag some brush to cover him." I stood up, starting toward a bushy limb, but reversed my direction and walked to Aunt Ada. I hugged her. Seeking her help had been the best decision. She patted my back. "We're either saints or fools," she whispered.

My excitement about saving the convict dwindled when I thought about climbing Yankee Hill after dark.

Picking up long dried branches, I kept a constant watch for
Indian spirits in the trees and snakes on the ground. In the
dark there would be no way of escaping either.

On our way down the hill Aunt Ada and I scouted a different route. It was a longer way but with fewer bushes and
longer patches of grass. We decided it would be an easier
path for the night move.

When we got to Aunt Ada's front porch, we collapsed in
cane-seated chairs and began to plan the night ahead, our
voices betraying our excitement. Aunt Ada said, "I don't
like the thought of bringing him into my house. We will
have to use the basement. I can lock the kitchen door that
leads downstairs." She looked at me. I nodded.

Aunt Ada pushed at her hair, and I stared hard at her.
She looked different. Her strawberry-tinged cheeks glowed
from time in the sun, and her eyes showed the same expression as when she talked about traveling to New York or
Japan. "Didn't do any good to spend all morning in the
beauty parlor, did it?" she said. That was the difference, her
hair. It was silver blond.

"You look like a movie star, like Lana Turner."

I chomped into the apple I'd picked off the tree in her
backyard and admired the snapdragon beds bordering the
porch. A spider's web stretched off the porch floor and up
to the pillar nearest the steps.

Aunt Ada leaned forward in her chair and crossed her
legs. A green moss stain dried on her dress. Her face held a

combination of expressions I had never seen before. She looked happy, excited; then her eyes flared, flooding sadness and fright into the iris, changing the color to deep-water blue.

Shadow sprawled out on her belly between two large pots of geraniums. She wagged her tail if we looked her way. It was the hottest part of the day, but a chill colder than wind off the creek at high winter settled around our chairs.

—Chapter Eight—

$\mathcal{I}$n front of the store, I jumped off my bike and propped it against the cinder-block building. The grocery stood at the fork of a road, where all the traffic coming into or out of town had to pass. Daddy said it was the best place in the world for a store. A white tin sign with hammered-out green letters spelled CARROLL, establishing our place in Morningside. The square building had a flat roof and twin-paned windows on either side of the front door. Bottle-green flower boxes, pouring over with red geraniums, adorned the windows, and a backless bench sat before each. A gas-pump island stood in the gravel parking area in front of the building. To the side of the store a horseshoe pit went unused, a testimony to Mama's absence. Weeds now poked up from ground formerly worn slick from feisty battles. Daddy had not set foot in the pit since Mama'd left, at the beginning of summer.

In no hurry to start loading cans onto shelves, I shilly-shallied around the gas pump, kicking at an occasional rock until Miss Dixie saw me. She stood by the cash register, near the window. "It's 'bout time." I moped into the store. "After you finish stocking up, I need help with these accounts." She screwed up her mouth to one side, like she had been chewing rhubarb, and struck an adding-machine key.

I worked sacks of cow feed into stacks and loaded the Pepsi cooler. The ceiling fan made a low humming noise. Miss Dixie tallied an account recorded on a fold-over tablet. The adding-machine keys clacked under her pounding, and the handle made a sputtering noise each time she released it for a total.

I was filling the Tom's Crackers jar with packs of cheese crackers when I heard an old truck pull up to the gas pump. I knew the rumbling sounds of Sardine Man's truck, but Miss Dixie had to look out the window to see who had arrived. Recognizing Sardine Man, she immediately lowered her head in official business. Without looking up again, she whispered, "You stay in here with me. That man gives me the willies."

I understood Miss Dixie's concern. I had seen Mama's uneasiness every time Sardine Man entered the store. Mama always greeted him in a low business tone, but Miss Dixie ignored his entrance.

Mama called him Sardine Man because his only purchase was canned fish. His true name was Otis Stiller, and he lived in a dingy shack on Mr. Hitcher's land, but no one knew where he was originally from. He had come to live in Morningside about the same time that Grandpa died.

Sardine Man talked about everything but himself, and he always tried to engage Mama in a debate. Once, during a horseshoe game, he told Daddy he had been a lawyer. Mama said Sardine Man was lonely and just needed somebody to talk to. Although she was uneasy with him around, she always obliged him with conversation. Daddy said he thought the old man wanted a family and had adopted us. The man's odd ways fascinated me, and the words he used sent me to the dictionary several times. His contrary nature made it difficult to determine if a good heart beat below the careless appearance.

One of my ambitions was to know more about Sardine Man. Mama got irritated with his speeches, but they impressed me. Somehow I wanted to find a sign of approval in his eyes. Most times he was engrossed in conversation with Mama, ignoring me no matter how many times I butted in. But I had no intention of disturbing him on this day. I would stay busy and pray he occupied himself with Miss Dixie, and above all, I prayed there would be no talk of the convicts.

Same as always, Sardine Man slammed the screen door so hard the metal Pepsi banner fell to one side. He swept across the cement floor, leaving a trail of dried mud, and sank into the wooden chair beside the drink cooler. A Philip Morris sign swung on a string above his head.

Pulling a pipe from his jacket pocket, he said, "Lady, do you think a just God would condemn a body to hell forever and ever and ever?"

My prayers were working. Sardine Man was going to give a speech about religion. I quickly glanced at Miss Dixie, and her dark eyes darted toward the unshaved man. He leaned back in the chair and fired the pipe, puffing smoke curls into the path of the fan's breeze. I followed Miss Dixie's lead and studied the man. His stained hands ended with each fingernail trimmed in a black rim. One of his laced boots had a tear near the tip of the toe. Although it was hot, he wore a jacket, its color bleached by too much time in the sun.

My attention was at full tilt. Miss Dixie couldn't stand anybody talking about the Bible or God. Sounding a little like Aunt Ada, she said, "We don't discuss religion in this store. If you want to know about God, go to church next Sunday."

Sardine Man grimaced and said, "Now, I suspect you go to church every Sunday, and you still avoid difficult questions. So I conclude there is little for me to learn in such an institution."

Miss Dixie let out a little huff, then buried herself in the accounts. She was silent, but a blush ran into her hairline and darkened her brown ears.

As if Miss Dixie had confirmed his statement, Sardine Man said, "Yes. Yes. Yes."

Not getting the anticipated response from Miss Dixie,

Sardine Man turned to me. I still stared at him. He said, "And have all those tomatoes been attended?"

"Yes," Miss Dixie said, without looking up. She didn't know he was asking me. I immediately got back to stocking the cracker jar.

Please let Miss Dixie's short answer halt his questions, I prayed. Questions about the tomatoes came too close to asking about the convicts. Just the thought of tomatoes or convicts churned my stomach. I was still feeling responsible for their escape.

"Suppose you haven't any idea of the whereabouts of the escapees?" I rested an arm on the open lip of the wide-mouth jar; my hand dangled inside it. Sardine Man started giving his opinions, trying to get an argument going. "I've often wondered why innocents run away. Or is that why they left: They were innocent?"

Sardine Man sounded genuine, but he had brought up what I wanted at all costs to avoid. I didn't fully understand the part about innocent people running away, but I guessed it had something to do with what Daddy always had said: "Every man is what you allow him to be." I realized everybody in Morningside knew about the convicts running away, but Sardine Man's interest seemed more mysterious to me. He might have seen me on Yankee Hill and figured out I knew something about the convicts, but I wasn't about to ask him.

"Now, you are going to be in the seventh grade. I hear you are bright, that you have read half the books in the school library." Heavy smoke rose from the pipe and wreathed his eyes. I quickly looked away from him, grabbing another handful of nickel-pack crackers and tossing them into the jar.

I felt him staring, so I said, "But I hope I don't get in Miss Frank's room."

"Is Miss Frank a liar?" he asked.

"No." I was shocked by his question.

"People lie in various ways, some just by saying nothing. Not telling what you saw could even be a lie." Sardine Man drew deep at the pipe.

"Miss Dixie says the truth will set you free." I tried to end the conversation. "Don't you, Miss Dixie?"

"I ain't getting into no such talk," Miss Dixie said. Her tone answered the question. "Do you want them canned fish?" she asked, standing up straight and bringing her hands to her hips. Sardine Man nodded, sucking his pipe.

The small storeroom was heavily stocked with extra canned goods. Wide shelves narrowed the walking space to a single, slender aisle. Several cartons had to be cleared so I could reach the one I needed. I was wrestling with two giant boxes when Sardine Man came into the room and blocked the doorway.

"You've got secrets," he said.

Over his shoulder I could see Miss Dixie straining to see into the room. "I don't." My response was weak and did not even convince me. Now I was sure he had seen me on Yankee Hill. It seemed he was trying to either warn me or get me to back down from my plan. I didn't care what his motive was, so I pushed my way around him and carried the box of sardines to the counter. Miss Dixie searched my face. "I have no secrets. I'm not a liar." I sounded convincing.

Sardine Man stood by the counter so close I could smell his vanilla-tobacco breath. Miss Dixie lifted her eyes from me and set them on the man. She said, "Now, what on earth makes you think a ten-year-old boy could have secrets?"

"Eleven," I corrected. Miss Dixie grunted like it didn't matter that she had forgotten my recent birthday.

Sardine Man pulled rumpled bills out of his pocket. "Oh, boys can have the darkest secrets of all." His voice was playful, like a game.

His words buzzed around my head like a pesky fly. I understood, and worse, I felt he knew what I was going to do and what I had already done. I shifted my weight from foot to foot, wishing he would take the fish and leave.

"Now, I want my purchase in a sack. I always want to view the products I am buying. I can't do that if a container conceals the merchandise. You folks should know my requirements by now." Sardine Man struck a match to rekindle his pipe. Miss Dixie arched an eyebrow.

"I'll do it," I volunteered to escape any further talk about lies or convicts. I also wanted to keep Sardine Man friendly toward me in case he knew Aunt Ada and I had been on Yankee Hill. Then a thought came to me that would please Miss Dixie and satisfy Sardine Man. "I would have to give you several bags for all the cans, but I could open the box; you could see the sardines and still use the box to carry the cans." Sardine Man nodded in agreement. Miss Dixie shook her head and went back to the accounts.

After Sardine Man inspected the canned fish, fingering each can, I picked up the box and used my back to push open the screen door. He was fast at my heels. Just as I cleared the door, Aunt Ada's Chevy stopped in the parking area next to the horseshoe pit. Sardine Man saw Aunt Ada step from the car and his eyes widened. He retraced his steps and sat again in the wooden chair.

Sardine Man's silent eyes followed Aunt Ada's every move, while I, still holding the box of fish, observed the store through the screen door.

When Miss Dixie saw Aunt Ada, she said, "Lordy, look at that hair."

Aunt Ada gathered soap, liniment, rubbing alcohol, and two cans of pork 'n' beans, bringing the assortment to the counter and standing in front of Miss Dixie. "I guess you mean my hair is pretty," Aunt Ada said. Miss Dixie giggled and shook her head.

"Better get some Teaberry gum, Aunt Ada," I said. She twisted her neck a little and shot her eyes around to glimpse at Sardine Man. She looked at me and winked.

"Two packs," she said, choosing the pink-wrapped gum from the neatly stocked candy display.

Aunt Ada carried the bag of supplies and tossed it on the car seat beside her. She waved like it was a normal day.

I stood in the shadow of a cloud, and heavier, slower clouds hung over distant mountains. *Please don't rain,* I said to myself. It was going to be difficult enough climbing Yankee Hill after dark; if it rained, it would be impossible.

Sardine Man rushed from the store. He said, "Watch out for liars. And watch out for yourself." He climbed into the truck. I shoved the box on the seat beside him. I did not look at him, because I thought my face might give away the secret of the hidden convict. Before he pulled out of the driveway, I returned to the safety of the store.

Miss Dixie and I talked a little about Sardine Man. She said, "He's just a crazy old man!"

I agreed with her and said, "Wonder why he buys all that fish?"

Neither of us had answers, so we busied ourselves with the late-afternoon customers who stopped at the store for tins of coffee and loaves of bread, or to use the telephone.

The Hitcher boys worked at the rayon plant and stopped once a week to fill their yellow Ford with gas. They always arrived just as we were closing the store, and they always smelled of beer. It was a safe bet one of them would ask when we were going to start carrying chewing tobacco. Of course Mama had no intention of ever stocking tobacco plugs; she had even considered discontinuing smoking tobacco—that is, until she realized the profits.

In preparation for the Hitcher boys, who Miss Dixie declared meaner than rattlesnakes, I neatly printed signs on cardboard-box tops: NO SPITTING. Then I taped the signs to both sides of the storefront. The Hitchers had a game of spitting their chews against the side of the store and betting on which stream of brown spit would hit the ground first. After each of their stops at the store, I had to scrub the tobacco stains off the walls.

I was too busy getting ready for closing to notice when they showed up. But I knew when Bell Hitcher burst into the store and threw himself on top of the Pepsi cooler. He pointed a finger at Miss Dixie, who was behind the counter.

"You're a brave nigger," he said. "I didn't know you people could write." My mouth was cotton.

"You got no call talking that way," Miss Dixie said, her voice quiet.

Bell jumped off the cooler. "Well, you ain't got no call putting them signs up." He was talking about my signs; signs Miss Dixie knew nothing about.

Edging out from behind the freestanding bread rack, I said, "She didn't do it. I did. And I did it because this is my daddy's store." Bell Hitcher stared at me. He shook his head and banged the screen door open with his fist.

"Well, I'll be damned," Bell said to his brother, but he spoke loud enough to be heard inside the store. "That boy that let the convicts loose is a nigger lover, too." They laughed, punching each other on the arm. "C'mon, let's try the screen door since they got our regular spots covered." Miss Dixie took the ax handle from under the counter and ran to the door.

I was afraid. "Let 'em do it, Miss Dixie. I'll clean it up."

She jerked the screen door open and held it with her back. She said, "That's four dollars for the gas." I stayed inside the store. Bell Hitcher's determined eyes sliced through Miss Dixie and bore into me. I felt his anger, but mostly I felt he would plan a way to get us back. Before he jumped into the yellow Ford and sped away, he threw four dollar bills on the ground and stepped on them.

"Don't pay no attention. Them boys ain't no good." Miss Dixie looked like she wanted to cry. She palmed the dollar bills, ironing them out on her dress. "Let's close up this place," she said.

Miss Dixie pulled the string on the overhead light. I flipped the OPEN sign to CLOSED and locked the door behind us. We waited for Daddy on the plank bench in front of Mama's flower box. Miss Dixie held a small bag of groceries in her lap. The thick clouds that had covered the distant mountains now hovered above and threatened to let loose any minute.

In a little while, Daddy's small truck buzzed to a stop in front of us. I leaped up to get my bicycle. "Looks like you just rescued us in the nick of time," Miss Dixie said. A pellet of rain ricocheted off the truck roof and struck Daddy's shirt pocket. Miss Dixie said, "Mister, you better leave that bicycle alone and get in the truck." Daddy nodded. I crawled into the seat beside him.

"Miss Dixie will get wet in the back," I said.

Daddy leaned out the window. "Miss Dixie, you get in

up here with us. It's gonna rain too hard for you to set out in it."

"I'll be all right."

Daddy stuck his arm and head out the window and yelled to the back, "Get in this truck, woman."

I whispered to Daddy, "Let Miss Dixie drive. Aunt Ada has been teaching her."

When Miss Dixie opened the door on my side of the truck, Daddy scooted toward me. He flipped his hand toward the steering wheel and said, "We're in your hands."

Miss Dixie hurried to the driver's side without any argument. I stretched forward to watch her. She grasped the wheel tightly in her strong hands. It began to rain hard. Drops splashed on the windshield like tiny water bombs. Daddy reached over and turned on the windshield wipers. Miss Dixie didn't seem nervous, even when she hit the shoulder of the road. Daddy said, "That's okay, just pull her back in the road." Miss Dixie did fine after that.

With the groceries put away, Miss Dixie started supper. I stood by the screen door and watched the rain flood the backyard. The pouring sound blocked out every other. Shadow huddled by the door, dodging the thunderous pelting at the edge of the porch. "Do you think this rain will let up soon?" I asked.

Miss Dixie looked over her shoulder and said, "Looks like a gully washer to me."

I pulled a chair to the door and prayed for the rain to

stop. Miss Dixie always preached that trouble does not come unless you go looking for it. Maybe that was what I had done. Did I seek this trouble? Was I getting into trouble so deep I would drown, like the grass in this storm? If I told Miss Dixie what was going to happen when full dark came, she would call it trouble. If I explained I found a wounded man on Yankee Hill and the discovery was an accident, she would say I had no business on that hill. She would say I looked for trouble and I found it.

It was seven o'clock. The evening light faded in the storm, making it seem later than it was.

I wandered from the kitchen into the living room.

Daddy slept on the couch with his glasses cockeyed on his closed face. Little snores circled his lips but got lost in the larger sound of the rain. The afternoon newspaper covered his lap, pinned to him by limp hands.

I tiptoed to his side, stifling an impulse to straighten his glasses.

A picture of Mama sat on an end table beside the couch and called to me. I forgot about Daddy's glasses and studied the silver-frame image of Mama. The photograph made her hair appear much darker than it really was. Her patient eyes almost spoke, almost asked me if I had finished the summer reading list, if I was ready for school to start. Mama smiled in the picture, but it looked like she didn't really want to. It was an encouraged smile, like someone behind the camera told her to smile and she did. Mama was not a smiling person. Daddy said she lost her sense of humor. The only times

I really saw Mama laugh was when Daddy snuck up behind her and rubbed his beard into her neck. She would let out a little scream and then laugh.

Behind the picture, a prized loving cup had turned brown around the edges. I fingered the silver trophy I had admired as long as I could recall: MISS DAIRY FARM QUEEN—1942.

Before Mama went to Winston-Salem, she and Aunt Ada spent long evenings in the living room, usually ganging up on Daddy about his choice of television programs. Mama and Aunt Ada refused to sit in the living room on Wednesdays when Daddy watched boxing. They retreated to the kitchen. But the last time the Miss America Pageant came on, Aunt Ada grabbed Mama's silver loving cup and ceremoniously presented it to Mama like she had the crown to go with it. I could tell Aunt Ada's fuss made Mama feel special.

I counted the weeks by the postcards Mama sent from Winston-Salem; every week, a new card, with Mama accounting for the weather and how much she missed me. Mama had been gone seven weeks, and I had seven cards to prove it. Neither Daddy nor Miss Dixie offered any explanation for her absence. I didn't care anymore why she went away, I only wanted to know when she would be home. I looked at Daddy, wanting to shake him awake and ask him when Mama would return. Instead, I turned back to the photograph.

— Chapter Nine —

$\mathcal{I}$ met Aunt Ada after dark. We had not counted on the downpour, and I was soaked. Aunt Ada wore a plastic raincoat with the hood pulled over her head. When she lifted her head, her face, outlined by the hood, lit up in the stream of light from the chrome flashlight she clutched. Her eyes held a quiet storm; her face shone with the brilliance of a spirit. I gripped the handle of the low wagon Aunt Ada decided to bring at the last minute. The wagon's usual purpose was transporting topsoil for Aunt Ada's snapdragon beds. My other hand melted into Aunt Ada's, and we began to climb Yankee Hill.

We fought our way up the familiar hill, which had turned foreign in the night rain. The path, slick with wet leaves, kept our feet sliding and made us feel like we were trying to skate backward. The bushy oak trees provided umbrellas, but when we made it to a clearing with only skinny pines above, the rain pelted us. My naked arms took the full impact of the piercing raindrops, and my eyes stung from the beating. I pulled free of Aunt Ada's hand and sheltered my face. The consolation the rain afforded was the absence of snakes. One other good thing about the rain— it would let the dried earth cement and fasten itself back together.

The thorns that snagged me earlier in the day now wilted in the rain. Aunt Ada lit our path so we could steer far beyond the reach of downed trees like the one that had speared my ear. I began to question each step up the dark slope. I had never heard of anyone climbing Yankee Hill at night. Perhaps we had been too hasty in this venture. Were Aunt Ada and I climbing the same path the convicts had taken last night?

Once we reached the plateau where the convict was hiding, Aunt Ada paused and squeezed my shoulder. Her touch confirmed that something important was happening. I tingled from the excitement.

We snatched up the camouflage erected earlier that day and tossed the branches and leaves into the woods. In the dark I could barely make out the man from the pile of brush. My hand accidentally caught his leg when I reached for one of the dead limbs. He bolted up, gazed at me for a moment, then immediately collapsed.

Side by side with Aunt Ada, I couldn't tell if it was the pounding of my own heart or hers I heard. When we finished uncovering the convict, Aunt Ada whispered, "Let's pull him up, slowly." We bent down on either side of the man, and at Aunt Ada's instruction I lifted his arm around my neck. His soaked armpit fitted onto my shoulder. With the dead weight resting on me and his fingers touching my arm, I breathed in the danger of our deed.

Like Sardine Man said, I had lied by omission and now had involved Aunt Ada in a scheme that could turn out more evil than anything I ever imagined. I was trembling with my own need to apologize to Aunt Ada, to convince her to run home with me and let this man, this convict, die or live or run away or go back to jail, where Miss Dixie had said he belonged. But I suspected that if we abandoned him, the man's fate would be left to Bell Hitcher.

Aunt Ada's life was at risk, as was mine. But saving this man, even if he was not worth saving, somehow re-sounded as important as our own lives. To my mind, I would be forgiven for telling Aunt Ada about the convicts hiding in Grandpa's house, and she would be forgiven for telling the sheriff.

"Can you lift a little harder?" Aunt Ada's sudden voice frightened me. Lost in my own thoughts, I had allowed the man to rest on me without trying to lift him. I straightened my legs, bringing the convict upright. The extra weight made my footing more unsteady. I could hardly stand.

We folded the man into the wagon and leaned his chest over his legs. His arms spilled over the sides. Aunt Ada retrieved them and tucked his hands into the sides of the wagon. I braced my knee against the wagon when it slipped forward under the weight of the convict.

For what seemed hours we labored down Yankee Hill. No guardian angel appeared to navigate the trail. I wanted to pray for strength, but I was not sure what we were doing was prayer-worthy. I relied on my own will and on Aunt Ada's direction, trying not to judge if what we were doing was right or wrong. Justification seemed to come in knowing our deed was not all good and not all bad. The human being we pulled behind us became my single strength.

By the time we reached Aunt Ada's house the rain had softened to a spatter. The basement door on the side of the house allowed full view of the road. While Aunt Ada fumbled with the door latch, I glanced over her shoulder and was surprised by a dark figure standing perfectly still in the road. I tugged at the plastic sleeve of Aunt Ada's raincoat. She glared at me. I motioned to the road. When she looked, the fire of a match sputtered like a burned-out firefly. Then we saw a small orange glow, like a pipe when first lit. We pulled tight to the door and froze.

When we dared to look again, the figure was gone. Later, Aunt Ada speculated that it was probably someone on his way to Mr. McCallister, who reportedly had a moonshine still, to get liquored up, as she put it. I guessed it might have been Sardine Man.

Getting the man out of the wagon was much easier than loading him into it. We jerked his arms, he plopped on us, and we struggled through the door.

I had been in and out of Aunt Ada's basement hundreds

of times, but easing down the steps this time seemed like the first. The shelves on the back wall, filled with canned tomatoes, corn, and peaches, seemed fuller. A bushel basket of empty jars sat in the corner, and a wood-burning stove and a small sink were on the same wall as the door. A cot sat under the stairs, which led up to the kitchen. The lone light in the room came from a small lamp posted on an upended orange crate. The Teaberry chewing gum from Aunt Ada's shopping lay beside the lamp.

Ducking under the open wooden steps, we maneuvered the convict onto the cot. Pain creased his face; every small movement caused his eyes to squint in agony. His hand crept up his side and clawed at the wound in his chest. Blood had caked into a ridge of reddish brown around the cut. The skin looked blue in the lamplight. The convict's fingers slid into one side of the wound, and he yanked the cut wider. I thought I saw a flash of white bone. Aunt Ada caught the convict's hand in hers. His fingers strained for freedom, then surrendered. Aunt Ada's caress told him he could rest.

Standing under the open stairs, I propped an arm on a step and rested my head. My wet shirt stuck to my back, and rain leaked out of my clothes, multiplying into puddles on the concrete floor. My only comfort came from the sound of three people breathing.

After removing her raincoat and drawing some water, Aunt Ada tore away the convict's shirt and washed his face. She guided the fresh washcloth over his chest, adjusting her stroke near the gaping cut. She worked the wet rag around the wound as if dusting one of the delicate porcelains she collected and displayed in the rooms above. When Aunt Ada squeezed the rag, the water in the pail turned pink. My stomach turned and I had to force myself to swallow.

Holding the rag toward me, Aunt Ada said, "Finish up while I get something to close the wound. Then we need to make sure he is warm; being out in the rain could cause hypothermia." She was at the top of the stairs before I could protest being left alone with the convict. I pulled back and stared at him. His breathing was easy, and his eyelids were still.

Aunt Ada had washed his face, arms, chest, and hands. The rest of his bath was left to me. I worked fast to finish before Aunt Ada returned, but I paused once to compare the man's body to my own. A few days before I turned eleven, I noticed the same fine hair below my belly button, and a little fuzz had begun just below my knees. The hair on the man's arms and legs was a light color, but coarse and thick. I wondered how long before my body would support the same.

I quickened the bath when I heard Aunt Ada's muffled footsteps nearing the basement door.

Aunt Ada emerged piecemeal on the steps. First her shoe came in view, then the hem of her skirt, her thin waist, her blouse, her chin, her full face, and her new blond hair, until she appeared, whole, at the bottom of the stairway. A green towel was draped over her arm, and both her hands were full of items gathered to doctor the convict. Pointing her elbow toward me, she said, "Take this towel and put it over him." She continued to the lamp and put down needle, threads, and her sewing box. I covered the convict and stood waiting for further instructions. The flame on a candle Aunt Ada lit caught my attention. She held a long needle over the open flame. Then she ran the needle through a cotton ball. The stinging smell of rubbing alcohol sobered me. I realized she was going to sew up the wound.

Walking toward me like an efficient nurse, Aunt Ada said, "You'll have to hold the skin together while I stitch it." She didn't bat an eye. I was ready to protest, but Aunt Ada assumed her position, expecting me to carry out my part. I had no time to think. My hands skated over the convict's chest, fingering hills of bone, until they reached the open wound. My stomach reached for my backbone. Without focusing directly on the wound, I squeezed the flesh together. Aunt Ada adjusted my hands, then brought the needle straight down. A river of warm blood streamed over my hand. I closed my eyes but snapped them open when the convict moaned and tried to jiggle away from the needle.

"Be still," Aunt Ada whispered, and the convict settled down and stayed in position until the stitching was finished.

Wiping her crimson-coated fingers, Aunt Ada leaned back as if she was admiring her stitches. She gently dabbed at the sutures with the stained towel, then dressed the wound with yards of white gauze. She arranged the convict's hands and drew a red-and-yellow Indian blanket over him. Her hands lingered at the blanket's ribboned edge, tucking it tight under the convict's chin.

Aunt Ada's preoccupation with nursing the convict disturbed me. I hadn't thought beyond getting him off Yankee Hill. What would we do with this man? Whatever calm I had managed up to that point began to wear thin.

I stood at the sink, letting the water run over my hands. It might have been the blood, but all of a sudden I was overpowered with the need to be clean. I scrubbed hard, wringing my fingers so tight they hurt.

I soaped my hands a second time. Miss Dixie believed in spirits. She had told me every time somebody that loves you passes away, you gain another spirit on your side. They all watch over you and pull together to keep you safe. The more people pass, the more protected you can feel. When Grandpa died, Miss Dixie said, "He's watching over you now, always on your side." If Grandpa watched, was he proud? Was he protecting me and Aunt Ada?

In an attempt to draw Aunt Ada away from her sickbed duties, I asked, "What are we going to do with him?"

I thought I detected concern in Aunt Ada's face. Or perhaps, like me, she had just realized the commitment we had made when we lugged the man into the basement. She said, "He's not ours, but we will have to decide what's best for him. He can help us make that decision." She left the cot and stood by the lamp. "Let's pray we have saved a man worth saving," she said to the wall before switching off the light.

I could almost hear Miss Dixie saying, "Anyone who asks for trouble, gets it." I hurried to Aunt Ada, who was halfway up the staircase. Over my shoulder I looked down at the convict on the cot. Let him be worthy, I thought.

Aunt Ada climbed to the light coming from the open door. She said, "If we need to take him to the hospital, well, let's worry about it tomorrow." She turned to me at the top of the stairs. "We are this man's only hope. His safety depends on us. No one must ever know he was on Yankee Hill or that he is here." I nodded, a little annoyed that she felt the need to question my ability to keep a secret. "He will have to stay in the basement. He can't leave, or he takes a chance of being discovered."

"He's our prisoner," I said.

Aunt Ada studied the pine knot on the doorjamb. She said, "He's his own prisoner."

— Chapter Ten —

Sleep had a hard time finding me. I warmed one pillow, then sought the cool one. My eyes were open when the first rays of dawn lightened the window, and I jerked upright in the bed. I sank back and rested against the headboard, the deed Aunt Ada and I had completed in the dark of night seeming even more scary in the fresh light of morning.

I told myself that this Sunday had to be like any other Sunday. I had to go to church, eat Miss Dixie's Sunday dinner, play with Shadow—no suspicion could be aroused by any act on my part. The windows brightened, bringing true color to the bedroom walls, and I jumped out of bed and hurried into the bathroom.

When I climbed into the bathtub, water sloshed around my body. I scrubbed to erase the traces of the climb up Yankee Hill. New scratches appeared on my arms, and two giant mosquito bites bulged on my neck. I had to be dressed before Miss Dixie saw me, to avoid questions about the scratches and welts.

Miss Dixie's version of "Peace in the Valley" filtered into the bathroom. She made up for missed notes with volume. "Mister, you in there?" her song stopped long enough for her to ask. She pecked lightly on the bathroom door. "Might be other folks wanting in there. You wouldn't want to be responsible for kidney failure."

I jumped out of the tub. Water splashed on the white tile floor and took two towels to soak up. Opening the door slowly, I listened to hear where Miss Dixie was. Her singing from down the hall indicated I could get into my own room and get dressed for church without being seen.

Fully dressed, I walked into the kitchen. Miss Dixie looked up from her cooking and said, "Well, you sure enough look eleven years old now. Don't you look just like a little preacher?" She referred to the necktie I wore. I always argued with Mama that none of the other boys wore them. Miss Dixie had no idea of the secrets I carried under the tightened shirt collar.

I squeezed into my usual chair at the kitchen table. Buttering a biscuit, I asked, "Where's Daddy? Is he going to church?"

Miss Dixie's head nodded toward the hall leading to Daddy's bedroom. "Your daddy's resting. I'm a little worried about him. He works too hard. You'll have to walk to church."

I did not argue with Miss Dixie, but I was going to walk to the store and retrieve the bicycle I'd abandoned in the storm the previous night. When I left the house, Miss Dixie was fumbling with the radio dial, trying to tune in to the preaching program that she sent money to every week. "Mister, be sure and close your eyes when you pray," she said.

When I got to church, Aunt Ada was playing the piano. She saw me and added zest to her already spirited "Bringing in the Sheaves." She wore a yellow-dotted dress with a high neckline and long sleeves to conceal any cuts from our climb up Yankee Hill. Preacher George leaned back in his tall chair, crossing his white stubby arms, which stuck out of a short-sleeved shirt. He craned his chubby neck and tilted to one side of the chair to peer at Aunt Ada's new blond hair. A chunk of his own heavily oiled hair fell on his forehead. Aunt Ada flipped her eyelashes a few times at him, then hit a sour note. I knew she did it on purpose, because she winked at me.

Preacher George had started at our church in late winter. Aunt Ada said the preacher inherited her. She had played piano at the church since she was little, and although neither she nor the preacher liked each other, she was determined to play piano for as long as she wanted. Aunt Ada said the preacher usually based his sermon on something he had seen her do. After he saw her sunbathing in short shorts and a halter, he blasted us with a sermon on shameless women with bare midriffs who tempted men.

The church smelled of pine oil and freshly lit candles. I took a seat at the end of a pew by an open window. The Hays sat in the row before me. Mrs. Hay was a big woman, and every time she stood up she threw out the back of her skirt. She reminded me of a cow switching its tail. It was warm and grew increasingly hotter as the preacher railed in a sermon about the lack of money to build a new parsonage. I guessed his new house was more important than anything Aunt Ada had done lately. Aunt Ada yawned a few times, which started a chain of yawners, including me.

Outside the open window, lazy oak leaves silently danced in the breeze. The graveyard ran beyond the trees and circled in back of the church. Grandpa's grave was two rows down from the top. I was trying to decide which was his tombstone when I saw Sardine Man propped against a low grave marker. He faced Yankee Hill, with his arms poised on his chest, a beard of pipe smoke circling his chin. His face wasn't clear to me, but something in the way he watched the scenery before him reminded me of the peace Easter brings.

The preacher banged on the pulpit and said, "Let us pray." Instinctively, my eyes closed so tightly I could see only purple wrinkles. I began praying my usual prayers. I prayed I would make the basketball team, but my more serious prayer, the one most likely to be answered, was that an undiscovered tick would not bury under Shadow's skin and give her black tongue. I ended every prayer with the request that I would be able to outrun any racer snake that took after me. But on that Sunday I added to my silent prayers. *Let the convict get better,* I prayed. *Let him be thankful we saved him, and please let him turn out to be a worthy man.* "Amen," I finished aloud. When I opened my eyes, I looked at Aunt Ada and wondered if her prayer was the same as mine. She flipped open some sheet music, and the congregation stood to sing the doxology. "Praise God from whom all blessings flow...."

I was first out of my pew and edged along the wall where the windows were, instead of taking the aisle. Excusing myself every time I stepped on someone's foot, I made it to the door and scrambled out the side of the church that faced the graveyard.

My hearty run down the slight hill made Sardine Man turn. "I saw you from the window," I said, nearing him. His hard eyes searched the church's stained-glass windows.

"That's eavesdropping," he said.

"Some people would say you are trespassing. You don't belong to the Methodist Church, but here you are on church property." I don't know where I got the nerve to say that. Ever since his visit to the store, I had wanted to talk to him. Maybe he would tell me what he knew or suspected about the convicts.

Sardine Man tapped his pipe on the side of the grave marker. He said, "You *are* bright. But this time you are wrong. I once belonged to the First Methodist Church of Asheville. That was before I decided to drop out of life."

"How can you drop out of life? You would have to die to do that," I said.

"You can just stop living the way you were. That's what I mean by dropping out," he said.

"I never heard of anybody dropping out," I said, puzzled.

"My view of life is different, and I speak the truth about it. Some consider me strange. That's because most people believe that all human beings must have the same aspirations. People can't accept what they don't understand, and they don't understand anyone that varies from what they know. I'm an enigma."

Enigma. Enigma. I repeated the word to myself so I could remember to look it up in the dictionary. "Why does Mr. Hitcher let you live on his land?"

"The only way I get around Hitcher is to stay my distance."

"Are you a relative of his?"

"I once did the man a favor, got his boys out of trouble, and now he provides me with a place to disappear." Sardine Man wore the same clothes he had worn to the store on Saturday, but his face was freshly shaven and his fingernails were clean. "Bell Hitcher and his kind are dangerous sorts. If you are planning to go against him, be careful."

I did not want him to think he scared me, so I said, "I know."

"To serve justice is noble, but caution is prudent. Never permit an unattended moment. Hitcher suspects the convict is hiding around here."

"And what do you think?"

"I think if you ever need me, I'll be there. I believe in justice, too."

Sticking her head out the church doorway, Aunt Ada yelled, "Austin, we need to speak before I leave for home."

Sardine Man tumbled off the tombstone. Down the hill a little ways from me, he turned and said, "One man cannot change the world, but united we stand a chance."

I ran to Aunt Ada. She gave me an extended hug. "What were you saying to that man?"

"Nothing." I had nothing to report. I was uneasy with Sardine Man's offer of help and thought it might upset Aunt Ada.

Either she found my talk with Sardine Man of no importance or she was preoccupied with concern for the convict in her house, because she started talking about him. She told me he had roused briefly but dropped back into deep sleep. The only thing she had learned from him was his name: Bass. We walked to her car, talking fast, hastily deciding that I was not to come to her house until dark. When people came near us, usually stopping to comment on Aunt Ada's hair, she would break our private conversation, smiling a Sunday smile to the intruders and waiting for them to be out of earshot before continuing. I wanted to ask if she could tell if the convict was worthy of being saved, but I was afraid to upset her. The truth was, I didn't want to know.

I had my bike upright and was straddling it when Aunt Ada yelled, "Austin, don't forget school starts tomorrow. I'll pick you up."

At twilight, with Miss Dixie sipping iced tea on the back porch and Daddy already in bed for the night, I jumped from my bedroom window and walked to Aunt Ada's. Misty lights lit the windows and made Aunt Ada's house look like a lantern. The night was warm, but a breeze forced my elbows into my belly. Lost somewhere in the crisp summer-turning-autumn night was the wishful belief that harm would never find me.

When Aunt Ada answered the door, I said, "Here's a shirt for him." I held out a red-checked flannel shirt I had retrieved from our ragbag. She did not say anything. We walked to the kitchen, she opened the door to the base-ment, and we descended the stairs.

The convict must have heard our footsteps, because his eyes fluttered and tried to open. When he finally got them open, he focused on me. I raised one eyebrow and gave him a proper mean look. Aunt Ada pointed to the shirt in my hand. "This is Austin; he brought you a shirt." The convict closed his eyes, then reopened them as if he was trying to signal in eye code.

Aunt Ada ran water in the pail we had used the night before. "Help me change the bandage," she said, motioning her head to the roll of gauze. I took the bandage and followed her to the cot, still holding the red shirt in the other hand. "Put the shirt down over there." With her eyes she pointed to a chair.

The convict pulled back when the water ran over the stitches. I pressed my teeth together. At the slightest touch he wrenched in pain and closed his eyes tighter. He might be dangerous, but he was too hurt to be a threat. With each stroke over the swollen wound the convict's body arched and stiffened. I stood back, getting involved only when directed by Aunt Ada. Mostly she had me cut strips of bandage. After I finished with the scissors, I hid them in an empty vase on a shelf over the sink.

I picked up a pack of Teaberry chewing gum and ripped it open. One piece slid out. I carried it to the convict and pressed the gum in his hand. He raised up a little so he could look at it. Then he smiled and hugged the gum between his fingers.

When Aunt Ada and I were back upstairs, we sat down at the dining table.

"Is he going to be well?" I asked, avoiding the real question of how long it would be before we found out if he was dangerous.

"The fever's down." Aunt Ada ran a hand through her hair.

I started to say something about planning to move him out of the basement when he could walk, but Aunt Ada reached a finger to my lips.

"Your mother was so beautiful when she carried you, before you were born."

Although it seemed Aunt Ada's mind was on the convict, I could tell she was avoiding talking about him. I said, "How could she have been beautiful? She was fat. She told me she had never been so fat. The day I was born she ate a whole watermelon."

"Pride. She knew how special you were going to be."

"How did she know? I could have turned out mean."

She sighed. "I guess women who have babies can tell. I'll never know for sure. Maybe it's the way the baby rests inside them."

"I wonder how the convict's mother felt before he was born." My eyes fixed on the door leading to the basement.

Aunt Ada looked at the door, too. Her lips curled into a friendly but sad smile. I wished I could read her mind.

—Chapter Eleven—

*A*unt Ada jumped out of the car, leaving the motor running. Miss Dixie appeared in the doorway of the screened back porch, and I scooted forward in my seat to see her hand. She held it out before her and pushed at the screen door with her crooked arm. Her hand was wrapped in an old towel.

Aunt Ada met Miss Dixie at the top of the porch steps, took her arm, and helped her down. I got out of the car and squeezed into the backseat. It would have been too hard for Miss Dixie to get into the back.

I always got scared when someone got hurt.

On the way to the hospital Miss Dixie said, "I hate you had to leave school on account of me. I would've been all right if I could have got the needle out." She adjusted her hand. "I never cared for that Sardine Man, but he was handy today. Saw me walking down the road and said he'd call you."

"It was lucky he came along. You don't have to worry now, Miss Dixie, we'll get your finger taken care of," Aunt Ada said, accelerating through a yellow traffic light.

I leaned forward on the back of the front seat and peered over at the hand resting in Miss Dixie's lap. "What happened?" I asked.

Miss Dixie lifted her hand off her lap. "I ran that sewing-machine needle right through my finger. Guess I had my mind on something other than my business."

Aunt Ada pulled her elbows into her side and swallowed hard. I pulled back a little ways from the seat. "How did you get your finger out of the sewing machine?" I asked.

"I yanked it from under that thing and broke the needle. I tried to pull the needle out, but I couldn't get at it. The worst part is I ruined them quilt squares I cut up last night," Miss Dixie said, lowering her hand back into her lap.

Miss Dixie spent her nights reading the Bible and cutting out quilt squares. She measured each piece of fabric with the top joint of her thumb, which she declared to be one inch long, and then cut the discarded shirts or dresses into perfect squares of differing sizes, depending on the pattern of the quilt she was making.

Nothing else was said until Aunt Ada stopped the car in front of the hospital. I knew the hospital because Daddy had brought me there before Grandpa died, taking me up to the second floor to visit him.

"This ain't the right place," Miss Dixie said, ducking her head to see under the sun visor.

Aunt Ada turned to face Miss Dixie. "This is the hospital, Miss Dixie."

"The white hospital. They don't take colored here."

"This is an emergency," Aunt Ada said, opening the car door and sliding out.

"Take me to the colored one." Miss Dixie nursed her hand to her breast.

"Don't be silly. Get out of that car right now." Aunt Ada shut the car door and waited.

Miss Dixie obeyed, but grumbled under her breath. I was crawling my way out of the backseat when Aunt Ada said, "Just stay in there, Austin. You don't need to see this." She chose calm words and pronounced each one more carefully than usual. She said, "I'll go in to support Miss Dixie, and you will stay in the car until I finish."

"I want to go in with you," I said.

"If a policeman comes along, tell him I'll be right back." She pointed to the EMERGENCY PARKING ONLY sign.

I waited until Aunt Ada and Miss Dixie made it up the steps and through the glass doors. Then I climbed out of the car and stood for a moment, looking at a grassy hill across from the hospital. Swings stood on top of the hill, shaded by huge trees that were brick-ringed and skirted with pink and red impatiens.

A wide wooden cross hung over the door of the red-brick hospital. I ran up the steps and stopped under it. Miss Dixie was at the far end of the hall, being assisted by a nurse. I opened the glass door and ducked into the nearby stairwell. From my one visit to Grandpa's bedside, I remembered the patients were on the second floor.

At the landing to the second floor, I listened for footsteps on the other side of the door. The silence let me step into the hall onto shiny white floor tiles that acted like mirrors, reflecting my own face back to me. The smell of alcohol and medicine bottles grew stronger with each step I took down the hall. When I reached the waiting room, several paned windows, dressed in thin gray curtains, lit the room with sunshine. From one of the windows, I could see a billboard over the Sunshine Bakery. Magazines were scattered on dull-green plastic chairs. I picked up a sports magazine and sat down.

I wanted to find Miss Dixie, but the hospital kept reminding me of Grandpa. When he was sick, I spent two hours in this room. Grandpa had never come home. I sat on the same chair and looked out the same window when he died. Maybe that was what bothered me, or it could have been the unnatural way the building seemed to breathe, a white breath in calculated rhythm. I wanted to run to every door and search every room until I found Miss Dixie and made sure she was not hurt. But I was scared—afraid Miss Dixie would be as pale as Grandpa had been when they took me in to see him. I did not want to see Miss Dixie pinned to a bed with an angel at guard, the way Mama said she saw Grandpa. She said the angel kept spreading its wings wider and wider until Grandpa disappeared in all the feathers, and she couldn't see him anymore.

Mama would have to come home from Winston-Salem now. Miss Dixie could not do the cooking and house chores with a bandaged finger, and if they kept Miss Dixie in the hospital, we would need Mama to watch for the angel.

Through a teardrop standing in my eye, the room grew as round as a fishbowl. Aunt Ada came in and sat across from me. She put her hand on my knee, but she didn't scold me for not staying in the car. "Miss Dixie is fine. Her finger is in a big bandage," Aunt Ada said. We sat in the waiting room for what seemed a long time, then went downstairs and got Miss Dixie and went home.

When we got home, Daddy was loading the car with a suitcase. He said, "So there you all are. I wondered if I had been deserted." He closed the trunk of the car and leaned against it. I rushed past Miss Dixie to tell Daddy what had happened.

Before I could get a word out, he pushed up from the car and smiled the deepest smile I had seen since Mama left.

"What's the matter?" I said.

"Everything's perfect. I decided to go get your mama. I'm on my way to Winston-Salem." I let Daddy hug me. He stepped around the car and sprang behind the steering wheel and was gone, leaving me behind. Not that I would have protested his going to get Mama, but if I had been given the chance, I might have asked to go with him.

Putting the last of the supper dishes into the sink, Miss Dixie peered out the kitchen window. "It's black as sin out there. Can't even make out your aunt Ada's house."

I was washing the dishes so Miss Dixie would not get her bandage wet. I looked up into the black window. "Not until the leaves fall. The woods are too thick this time of year."

Still staring out the dark window, Miss Dixie said, "I'm surprised she's not scared to death to stay out here in the country all by herself. Pretty woman like her should have married long ago."

Aunt Ada was the bravest person I knew. And if Miss Dixie knew about the convict, she would think so, too. Keeping up the conversation kept my thoughts off Daddy and Mama, so I said, "Aunt Ada never had a boyfriend, so how could she get married?" I finished the last dish, sat down at the table, and propped up my head with my hands, trying not to appear sleepy.

"Oh, yes, she did." I figured by staying quiet, I could get Miss Dixie to continue. "That's what drove her off to teachers college. He was a handsome thing, but he had ways. A baseball player. Can you believe that? Said his job was playing ball. A man ain't got no business playing a child's game once he's grown."

"Did he play for the Asheville Tourists?"

"Well, he could have. The point is, he was lazy. Didn't know what an honest day's work was. But he turned your aunt's head. She was crazy about him. Nobody could talk any sense into her. Your grandpa even beat her with a razor strap for sneaking out to meet him. But do you think that would stop her? No, she said there was nothing anyone could do or say to stop her from seeing Joe. Joe Winter, that was his good-for-nothing name."

I thought Miss Dixie might be making up this story to get her mind off her injured hand, so I said, "How do you know this story? You only came to work for Mama after I was born."

"Well, Mister, I used to do day work for your grandpa. You know my mama used to keep house for him, and when she passed, I took up the job. That's how I know, Mister Smarty-pants." Miss Dixie dried the last dish, slid it into the cabinet, and laid the drying rag on the counter.

She looked at me. "Why am I telling you this story?" Then quickly dismissing her own question, she said, "Well, it's history. Everybody knows it."

I wanted to hear the end of the tale, but was afraid Miss Dixie was going to clam up because I had questioned her credibility. I asked, "What happened to Joe Winter? Does he still play ball?"

"Lord knows what that man's doing. He asked your aunt Ada to marry him. Everybody figured he was after your grandpa's land, everybody except your aunt. She set out to marry him. She bought a fine dress—I helped hem it—and was planning with the preacher for the church. But your grandpa said he wasn't having no such wedding in a church he helped build, on ground he gave for holy purposes. So that woman"—Miss Dixie pointed to the window—"stubborn as she is, said she was going to run off to South Carolina. That was before she found out what a good-for-nothing she was messing with."

I had seen a picture of Aunt Ada and a man I now figured was Joe Winter in Mama's cigar box of photographs. The man in the picture was tall, with curly, dark hair and a flashy smile. Aunt Ada and the man stood before a bushy tree and looked into the camera. He had his arms around Aunt Ada's waist, pulling her tight to him.

"I guess that soured your aunt Ada on men."

"What soured her?" I asked.

Miss Dixie's eyes reflected in the kitchen window. She appeared to be seeing a picture. "Now, I don't know this for sure, I wasn't there. Your mama told me this story. She said it happened in early spring, right before the flowers started blooming. I can just guess how Joe Winter turned your aunt's head with those flashing eyes of his. Anyway, your aunt Ada climbed up the hill to the McCallister place, just wandering around on a perfect day."

"I know that house. McCallister sells moonshine," I said, scratching my neck and trying not to yawn.

"They say he does. That house was never looked after; I even heard they let chickens roost in the kitchen. Well, when your aunt got up to the house, a dark-haired girl come out and asked her what she wanted. This girl was real pretty, your mama said. Your aunt Ada was surprised, because she didn't know any women lived up there with all the men."

My eyes closed a couple of times, but I was interested to hear the rest. I pulled up straight and tried to shake the drowsiness out of my head. Miss Dixie was so involved in telling the story, she did not notice I had nodded.

"About the time your aunt was going to introduce herself, like a lady's suppose to, a little boy came out of the house and hugged the girl around the legs. And then from behind the woodpile up stands Joe Winter. That little child ran to him, yelling, 'Daddy, Daddy.'" Miss Dixie shook her head from side to side and stared at her bandaged finger.

"Your aunt Ada never saw Joe Winter again. But in a few days, we heard he had left town with the girl. It hurt your aunt, tore a hole in her heart so big no love could stay in it. The very next week, she went up to Virginia to stay with your mama. Then she went to teachers college. She didn't come back home for three years."

Miss Dixie hunched forward, squinted, and strained to read the stove clock. "Look at the time. You get right in bed, but don't forget your prayers." She touched my cheek with her good hand. On my way to bed, I heard her say to herself, "I hope and pray none of these country bugs get on me."

With a quilt pulled around my neck and with the comfort of Miss Dixie puttering around in the other rooms, I thought of Aunt Ada and Joe Winter. I hoped Aunt Ada's heart had healed back up and she could love again. When tomorrow came, I would get the picture from Mama's cigar box and add it to my rainy-day collection.

— Chapter Twelve —

I was searching Daddy's closet for pants to take to the convict when Miss Dixie called from the kitchen, "Mister, that nasty-mouthed little girl is skating on the back porch. You'd better get out there and calm her down before she scratches the paint." It had to be B.J. She was the only person in Morningside with roller skates.

I grabbed two peanut-butter cookies on my way through the kitchen, offering one to B.J. when I got to the porch.

"She make them?" B.J. asked, watching Miss Dixie through the screen door.

"Yeah," I said, my mouth full of cookie.

"Well, I wouldn't eat nothing a witch made," B.J. said, pushing the cookie away from her. She skated in circles in front of the screen door. Even when she stopped skating, she zoomed the rollers back and forth over the porch floor. I sat down on the edge of the porch and was glad B.J. followed my lead. I felt Miss Dixie was getting madder by the minute about the skates.

"Miss Dixie has got powers. She can remove warts by talking to them, but she's not a witch."

"What do I care about her powers. I don't care a thing about her." B.J. looked to the far end of the tomato patch. "My daddy said old man Hitcher's boys are hunting for the convicts," B.J. said.

"The convicts are in Tennessee by now," I said.

"I don't want them old hell-fire Hitchers to catch them, anyway. I want my daddy to catch them."

B.J. tugged at the edge of a dirty Band-Aid encircling her index finger. "That turtle nearly bit the crap out of me. I jerked my finger out of its mouth just before it chomped down."

Miss Dixie stood at the screen door. I looked round to see her wiping her hands on a dish towel, but B.J. did not know she was there. "Little girl, ain't you ashamed to be cursing like that?"

At the sound of Miss Dixie's voice, B.J. jumped up, stood in the grass, and faced the screen door. She stuck out her tongue at Miss Dixie, who was on the porch by now. Miss Dixie leaned forward and stared down at B.J.

B.J. took a heavy step backward and said, "Everybody round here knows you're a witch."

Miss Dixie sat down in one of the high-back rocking

chairs and began a gentle pedal. She softly raised her eyes and in a real sweet voice said, "Why don't you stay the night? We ain't had a redheaded girl in this house before."

B.J. shook her fingers like they were on fire. She stretched her neck and scratched it. "Quit looking at me. You're making me itch."

Miss Dixie held out her hand. "Come here and let me rub it."

"No damn witch's hands are touching me. Hell, I'm getting away from here." B.J. skated across the backyard and turned the corner of the house.

When she was out of sight, I started laughing and could not stop. I bent over, holding the peanut-butter cookie close to my chest. I flopped off the porch's edge and sprawled on the fresh grass with the cookie smashed under me. My laughter was contagious, and Miss Dixie caught it.

I was still laughing when something hit me in the back. I looked at Miss Dixie, who was scrambling out of the rocker. "What's so funny, baby boy? What are you and your mammy laughing at?" I recognized Bell Hitcher's voice about the time he straddled me and leaned forward, pushing his sharp chin into my neck. I bucked up, trying to shake him off me. "Get up, horsie," he yelled, pushing his hips into my back and tightening his knees at my sides.

"Get off that boy," Miss Dixie yelled.

I pushed flat to the ground and then bucked up with all my strength. I thought I had bounced Bell Hitcher off me. He slumped to my side. I jumped up and saw B.J. standing over the man. She said, "Saw him sneaking up here, so I doubled back."

"He's always sneaking around," Miss Dixie said.

Bell was dazed. "B.J., what did you do to him?" I asked.

"I kicked him in the head with my skate."

"She sure did," Miss Dixie said.

Bell pulled his head up and shook it in slow motion. He struggled to his feet. I pulled back to the porch. B.J. continued to stand near him. She said, "Get on home, Bell Hitcher. Get your tail off this land." She put her hands on her hips. "And"—B.J.'s voice got louder—"my daddy said if you ever throw another rock at me, he's coming over to beat your butt."

Bell swayed away from us. He raised his arm and made a fist. "Watching, always watching you," he muttered.

B.J. propped against the edge of the porch. "He ain't nothing to be scared of. He's dumber than me. But his brother, Elmer, is cute, almost looks like Elvis Presley. My mama said if Elmer Hitcher was washed up, he'd be a good-looking man."

"Shoot, looks ain't what makes a person good or bad," Miss Dixie said.

B.J. sat down on the porch and braced her back on one of the pillars. "I'll take one of your cookies now, Miss Dixie."

"Sure enough," Miss Dixie said, opening the screen door.

"Do you think Bell Hitcher knows where the convicts are hiding?" I asked B.J.

"If anybody knows, it's him. He's always nosing into other people's business. He shimmies up trees and hides in the leaves. That's where he throws rocks at me. He hit my bike. And here"—B.J. pulled up the leg of her shorts to expose a bruise—"he hit me."

Shadow came over the ridge from the creek, stopping and shaking creek water out of her fur before she came across the tomato patch toward us. Bell Hitcher saw her and paused at the edge of the field to aim a silent finger. Then he jerked around to face B.J. and me. He raised his hand and said something, but he was too far away for us to hear.

The next day on the way home from school, Aunt Ada said, "When we get to my house, you go on in the basement and help Bass get cleaned up. Give him the clothes you brought."

I hesitated before agreeing. I dreaded being alone with the convict, but Aunt Ada's calling him Bass, instead of referring to him as the convict, gave me new courage.

Walking into Aunt Ada's house, I dropped my schoolbooks on the breakfast table and hugged the bag of clothes to my chest. I stared at the door leading to the basement, listening to Aunt Ada in her bedroom. Unlocking the door and holding the doorknob in my hand, I announced, "I'm going to the basement now." I raised my voice to be heard in the house and in the basement. Carefully, I propped the door ajar behind me.

Halfway down the stairs, I could see the cot. It was empty. I quickly scanned the basement, scrunching my neck and lowering my head to search far corners. The convict was nowhere in sight. Bass had either left the basement or he was under the staircase, out of my view. After waiting until my pulse calmed and my normal breath returned, I walked down the stairs. Once fully in the basement, I pivoted to the wall under the stairs.

Bass leaned on the sill of the small shuttered window, and the incoming light striped his hand. He turned at the rustling of the paper bag I carried and moved away from the window. With one hand he rubbed at his temple, and the fingers of his other hand moved over his face, surveying the shape of it. Then, with a flat hand, he trailed down his throat and let his hand continue roaming over his chest, brown from long days in the sun. His hand avoided the lumpy bandage that covered his heart side. When he did accidentally touch the covered wound, he threw his head back and clenched his fists. Muscles bulged in his neck. Once recovered from the pain, he examined his body as far as his hands could reach. I lowered my head, fearful our eyes would meet in embarrassment.

I held out the paper bag I had dutifully brought him. He accepted it without a word. Rummaging through the clothes selected from Daddy's closet, he found the gray trousers and quickly covered himself. After the pants were zipped, he extended a hand to me and said, "Thanks. I know you're Austin. My name's Bass." I shook his wide hand but kept a full arm's distance.

"There's a shirt here somewhere. A red shirt. I brought it on Sunday."

"Would you grab that liniment and give me a rub?" Bass hobbled to the cot and lay flat on his stomach, careful of his injured side.

My hand gripped the brown bottle, but I remained in place across the room from the cot. The bottle stuck to my fingers.

"I got more aches than you'll ever have in a lifetime," he said, propping his chin on folded hands. "You got to be careful not to run the stuff round on my side. That wound is tender, and liniment in it would send me through the roof."

"You're glad Aunt Ada and I saved you, aren't you?" I asked, kneeling down beside the cot and loosening the bottle cap. I leaned back to avoid the strong fumes.

Bass rolled his head to one side and looked at me. "I guess so." He must have sensed my uneasiness, because he added, "Sure. I'm proud you and your aunt saved me."

I rubbed and Bass talked. He told me about Atlanta, where he grew up. I told him I had been there and to Charleston and to Daytona Beach. He said he had been to Washington, D.C.

"Daddy said we can't go up there until the Democrats take over the White House," I told him. That made Bass laugh. He straightened up and pulled at his chest. Laughing made the skin stretch at the wound.

Aunt Ada had told me my mind should be like a box with compartments—each holding special information that might not be needed every day but would always be there to pull out when needed. I knew there would never be anything in my rainy-day box as important as the treasures of this moment, this summer. I tried to record each separate instant in my mind.

When Bass rested again, he rolled on his back and stared in my eyes. "You're a trusting boy. How do you know I'm not a murderer? How do you know I wouldn't kill you and your aunt and steal everything?"

I was startled at first. Fiddling with the liniment cap and taking a long time to match the grooves of the jar and lid, I said, "My daddy believes we get gut feelings about people."

"Is your daddy out there hunting me?"

"No, Daddy's in Winston-Salem." I bit my tongue for letting that slip. Bass might feel he had the upper hand if he believed Aunt Ada and I were alone. I tried to recover by saying, "Miss Dixie—she's our housekeeper—is real good with a gun."

I straightened my back and stared at Bass. Mischievous eyes stared back, but his face showed no intention of harm. He smiled and said, "You mean an old colored mammy is going to take care of all of us?"

"Miss Dixie's not that old," I answered.

Bass's smile dried and allowed a somber mood. "I'm a convict, an escaped convict."

"Daddy trusted you. But Miss Dixie thinks Daddy trusts too many people." I got up from the floor and returned the liniment to its place on the table. Somehow I was not afraid. I said, "Maybe Aunt Ada and I are trying to do what we learned in church. Everyone needs help now and then. We're just helping."

"I'm not going to hurt anybody, never have," Bass said.

Trying to change the subject, I said, "Is *Bass* a normal name in Atlanta?"

"Named after my mama's people. It was their last name. My mama said she didn't want the name to die out, and made me promise to give it to one of my own."

"Me too. I mean, Mama named me Austin for the same reason. She doesn't have any brothers."

"So your aunt's name is Austin?"

"Ada Austin."

Bass propped up on his side and massaged the hair under his arm. "How much danger is your aunt in, having me in her house?"

"We don't think about that."

"Who else lives around here?"

Aunt Ada swept down the steps. Bass hunched up his shoulders and pulled back, turning his face away from her. I spotted the red shirt and took it to him.

"No one lives on my property but me. I own Yankee Hill, the place Austin found you."

Bass sat up on the cot and started to pull on the shirt. He must have hurt his side, because he dropped the shirt and coiled his arms over his chest. Aunt Ada rushed down the steps and over to the cot.

"Have you ripped the stitches?" Aunt Ada lifted the shirt from Bass's lap and flung it in a corner. Bass fell back on the cot. A fine line of blood seeped through the bandage and began broadening across the white linen.

"Austin, get some water," Aunt Ada said, tugging at the bandage. I brought a pail of water and set it beside her. She finished removing the blood-spotted dressing and handed it to me. I closed my eyes, but not quick enough. With clinched eyelids, I tried to dismiss the line of red blood oozing from the swollen pink wound.

When I looked again, Aunt Ada had redressed the cut and Bass's hands rested in a tranquil clasp.

"Bell Hitcher chased you up Yankee Hill," I said.

"Austin, let's not talk about that right now." Aunt Ada sounded uncomfortable.

"It was him and his brother and his daddy."

Aunt Ada stared at me in silence. Then she turned to look Bass straight in the eye. "We don't know who chased you and the other man. Whoever they were, they were wrong."

"I showed the tattooed man the way to Canton."

A sadness clouded Bass's gray eyes. "I hope he made it away from these hills."

"Did he steal Daddy's shoes?" I asked.

"I reckon so," Bass said, closing his eyes. "He dropped them running from the fire."

"The shoes were on our porch the day after the fire. Bell Hitcher was there, too. He must have found them," I said.

Aunt Ada put her hand on Bass's shoulder. Without opening his eyes, he rested his chin on her fingers.

One evening about a week later, when Bass's injuries were greatly improved, the three of us played Chinese checkers in the basement. I think that was the night Aunt Ada began to truly trust Bass.

A marble tumbled from Aunt Ada's side of the table and rolled to the far wall. Bass hopped out of his chair and retrieved it. He came back to the board and stood over Aunt Ada. "Your checker, miss," he said, offering the green marble. It must have been the tender way he laid the sparkling agate in her palm, because Aunt Ada's profile softened with the gesture. For the first time I saw Aunt Ada give Bass the look that was so familiar to me, a look she reserved for those few of us who were allowed to be close to her.

Bass appeared shy and leaned on the back of the empty chair. He avoided Aunt Ada's look and stared at the wall. He said, "I wish we were in Atlanta." Aunt Ada and I stared at him. "I mean, so we could go out and celebrate."

"Celebrate what?" I asked.

"Celebrate you and me and Chinese checkers." Bass reseated himself at the checkerboard. "Celebrate being alive."

—Chapter Thirteen—

The next day, after I had carried Bass's supper to the basement and helped him find a piece of the plastic model ship
I had given him, I hurried home to my own supper with
Miss Dixie. The wind scooped up some fallen leaves, scuttling them over the dying grass. One caught on my shoe. I
pulled my arms tight across my chest to ward off the chill.
Daddy's hounds were restless when I passed their pen, so I
stopped for a moment to assure them Daddy would be
home soon. I was sure they missed him as much as I did. In
reality, I did not know when Daddy would be back from
Winston-Salem. He had been gone only a couple of days,
but every day his return seemed farther away.

   Seeing the dogs reminded me I had not seen Shadow all
afternoon, but I figured she was at the creek taking her
daily bath and would be waiting for me on the porch when
I got home.

I cleared the woods, all usual fears of encountering a snake lost to memory. Dusk darkened the path, and the fields turned a hazy gray. A few red spots on droopy vines highlighted the harvested tomato patch, and a desperate bird picked over the spoiled fruit, searching for seeds. Crossing Mama's faded summer garden, I stopped to kick at a stubborn vine. That's when I saw Sardine Man. He emerged from the woods at the far side of the tomato field holding something in his arms. I moved closer and saw clearly he carried Shadow.

Answering my yells, Miss Dixie hurried out the back door and stood on the porch. I ran to Sardine Man. He gently lowered Shadow into my arms. A handkerchief was tied round the top of her head.

"Somebody shot her." Sardine Man pulled back. I looked at his face, silently questioning if he had killed my dog. Tears stood at the edges of his old eyes, and his cheeks were wet. A tear rolled from his chin and landed on a cocklebur tangled in Shadow's white fur. "Senseless," he said, raking a shirtsleeve over his eyes. I stared at the dog in my arms. She lay limp and heavy like a broken toy.

Miss Dixie was running across the field, screaming loud. I looked round as she neared me. Aunt Ada was coming out of the woods, Bass behind her. I supposed they were alarmed by Miss Dixie's screams. Bass ducked behind a pine when he saw Sardine Man, but I had seen Bass. I was sure Sardine Man had seen him, too.

Shadow was heavy. I sat down, holding her. Miss Dixie

and Aunt Ada stood over me, silent but huffing for breath, and Sardine Man vanished into the woods. Bass circled round the field, hopscotching from tree to tree. He walked behind me, and I felt Miss Dixie pull away at the sight of him.

Aunt Ada said, "Come on, Miss Dixie, let's go in the house." Leaning on each other, they left the field. Miss Dixie kept looking back at Bass. Aunt Ada turned at the porch steps to yell, "Bass, the spade is in the basement."

I carried Shadow to the tire swing, then to my bike. The duck quacked near the porch. Her song was sad and low.

After Aunt Ada and Bass had gone, I sat down in Shadow's favorite spot. She had dug out the grass under Mama's peach tree to make a midday bed. I reached up and hooked an arm over a low limb, watching the western sky change from dark purple to night.

In the absence of playmates, except for B.J., Shadow had been my best friend. Everybody liked her, even Mama, who thought animals should stay in their place. She shooed Shadow off the porch all the time, but Mama would miss Shadow. Daddy would, too, even if he did prefer hunting dogs over pet dogs. But I would miss Shadow most.

Miss Dixie came out on the porch, and I expected her to yell for me to come inside. Instead she walked to the peach tree and sat down beside me. "It was good of that man to help dig the grave," she said.

I was still angry about Shadow getting shot and was

blaming myself. "He's an escaped convict," I said, partly to shock Miss Dixie and partly to put some of the blame for Shadow's killing on Bass.

Miss Dixie tried to appear brave, but she kept jerking up at sounds reaching out of the darkness. I kept trying not to cry and to be strong like Daddy and Bass.

"He's one of the convicts that ran away from the tomato patch," I said. "He's been hiding in Aunt Ada's basement."

"I suspected something strange was happening, the way you been sneaking around. Your aunt Ada filled me in how you-all found him up on Yankee Hill."

"You're afraid, aren't you, Miss Dixie?"

"Maybe a little." Miss Dixie's voice was real low and she sounded sincere. "But I know the Lord watches over us."

"Are you going to tell the sheriff or Daddy?"

"I ain't gonna think about it. You just keep him out there." Miss Dixie pointed toward Aunt Ada's house.

When we both got quiet, and Miss Dixie stopped jumping at noises and became peaceful, I cleared my throat to get rid of any sounds of being choked up. "Do you think dogs go to heaven?" I asked.

"I reckon the Lord will take the good ones in. And Shadow, well, she's gone there, sitting right beside your grandpa." Miss Dixie's respect for the dead brought me comfort.

Leaning back in the hole Shadow had dug, a bone she had buried stuck in my leg. I dug it out and held it up for

Miss Dixie to see. She said, "I can remove warts with that."

Shadow had left her treasure. She must have known I would find it. I looked at the black sky and knew it was going to be a moonless night.

—Chapter Fourteen—

$\mathcal{M}$iss Dixie took enough clothes to spend several days at her cousins'. I was convinced she wanted to be away from convicts and storekeeping for a while.

I moved in with Aunt Ada. On my first day of staying with her, Daddy called. He said Mama looked great and was fine, but when I asked to speak with her, he said she had gone shopping. It was good to hear Daddy's voice. His call cheered and excited me that he would soon be home.

The next day, I stopped after school at my house to pick up clean clothes. The sparkling white kitchen, usually animated with Miss Dixie's cooking chores, was dead quiet. I spotted the black walnuts Miss Dixie had pestered me to hull. She and I had gathered them down by the creek bank near Grandpa's old house. Miss Dixie planned to make a fresh-apple cake as soon as I hammered out two cups of nuts.

I cracked the nuts and cleaned away the shells and newspaper, then headed for Aunt Ada's. I took the road instead of the path through the woods. As I approached Aunt Ada's house, I noticed Sardine Man's old truck. It was parked in the curve on the other side of Aunt Ada's house. The only place I had seen the truck parked before was at the store.

I backed into the basement, turning to face the room after I had closed the door. Aunt Ada stood against the cement wall, and Bass stood to the side of the stairs with his arms out of sight. Streaks of afternoon light streamed through the fastened shutters. When my foot touched the first step into the room, Bass jumped forward and grabbed my arm. He threw me against the wall next to Aunt Ada. I dropped the clean trousers I carried.

"What are you up to?" Bass bellowed. His voice was deeper than I had known. His eyes widened. I was speechless and could manage only small tufts of breath. "Whose truck is out there? Did you plan something on your own?"

His questions were like bullets. I turned to face Aunt Ada in a plea for explanation. She moved away from the wall. Bass raised his hand. "Stay put," he said.

Aunt Ada ignored the command. She moved away from him and sat in the ladder-back chair she had brought from upstairs. Without looking at me or Bass, she said, "This is my house. This is my basement. That is my yard." She pointed to the door. "Beyond the yard is a road. I do not own the road."

Bass squatted before the chair. "Whose truck is that, and why is it parked so close to *your* yard?"

Regaining a somewhat natural breathing pattern, I said, "It's Sardine Man's truck—I mean, Otis Stiller's. I saw it when I came up the road."

Bass turned his head toward the wall where I was cowering, then looked back at Aunt Ada.

Aunt Ada raised her head to face Bass. She must have read a question in his look, because she said, "He's an old man who lives down the road, an odd but harmless old man." Bass continued to stare at her. She shifted in the chair. "Who knows why he is out there parked in the road? But you can be assured that neither of us summoned him."

Bass bent his head and rubbed his forehead. "I'm going crazy cooped up in here. I wake up with sweat running in my eyes. My ears ringing with shotgun blasts. I can't even get my breath sometimes."

Aunt Ada crossed her legs. She leaned forward and said, "I can understand how difficult it is to be confined. But to doubt our trust..." She pulled up straight in the chair and continued. "Questions circle me all the time. I can be in the middle of an arithmetic lesson and my mind rattles, asking me what I am doing risking two innocent people for the sake of a man I hardly know. I trust the right decisions have been made, and you have to trust us. The people in your nightmare would not stop with you. Austin and I share the danger."

The cold cement chilled my back. I felt betrayed. From

the night I helped drag Bass off Yankee Hill, he had consumed every afternoon of my life. I soothed his back with liniment rubs, dressed the scars he would carry to his grave, talked to him about anything he wanted to discuss, and even gave him my best model ship kit, which I had saved from last Christmas. How could he question me?

Aunt Ada finally rose from the chair, walked to the small lamp on the orange crate beside the bed, and punched in the switch. The beam funneled through the shade and lit her face in ghost white. I hurried to her side.

Turning to Bass, she said, "Austin made a map for you. We have been planning for you to get away from here. Show him the map, Austin."

Aunt Ada looked to me for confirmation. I hesitated. It was time to learn about Bass. Why were we questioned about sincerity when we knew nothing of this man except what he wanted to expose? Real questions needed to be settled. Instead of producing the carefully constructed map, words flipped off my tongue so fast I shocked myself. "Why are you here? Why were you in jail?" The sound of my own words hung in the room like someone else had spoken them.

Bass rubbed his eyes. He sank into the chair vacated by Aunt Ada. I watched him yank at a loose thread in the gray pants I had brought him. I shook with the anticipation of learning his story. When Aunt Ada spoke, I was surprised she did not share the anxiety. She said, "Now, Austin, we don't have to know Bass's personal business." Personal business. I thought Aunt Ada had gone crazy. I studied her face. Unvoiced questions appeared in her quieted eyes. Had we drawn too close to terror? Had we truly run headfirst into our own trap? Maybe she was signaling me to pending danger.

The room was so still I could hear a squirrel scratching in the yard, probably looking for an acorn. Bass looked above his head at the raw wood beams, then he slowly lowered his head to face me. A sharp spear of light jetted through a shutter and struck his right eye. "The boy is right. You should know who you saved."

Moving toward the stairs, Aunt Ada said, "We don't need to know anything. Truth is not always meant to be told." I could not believe my ears. Aunt Ada had always been as curious as I, and now she wanted to ignore the important facts this man was willing to give. My mouth was open and ready to protest, but Bass read my mind.

"Well, no glamour to what happened with me." I figured he was stalling and was going to take Aunt Ada's invitation to wiggle out of telling the truth. I crossed my arms. "I got put in jail for fighting. Just a plain old fistfight with regular good old boys." He raised a finger to correct himself. "Good old *drunk* boys."

I understood his every word and every gesture, but I rejected the idea of someone being put in jail for fighting. He must have wounded someone in the fight.

"See? Now we know," Aunt Ada said. She planted one

foot on the steps that led upstairs. I pulled back, tightening my arms. I would not follow her lead.

"Oh, they don't put drunks in jail for fighting," Bass said. I uncrossed my arms. "No sir, one of the old boys was your sheriff's son. He wasn't hurt much, but the sheriff got mighty sore and said somebody was going to pay." Bass turned the chair around and straddled it, gripping the spokes of the ladder-back. "That was in January."

"What happened at your trial?" Aunt Ada asked.

"Trial? No trial. Things don't work like that when the sheriff decides to teach somebody a lesson. I became a prisoner without a sentence. That's why I ran away, left the tomato patch. I didn't want to spend the rest of my life as free labor. I figured I'd been in jail long enough for fighting, so I let myself out," he said, staring into Aunt Ada's face.

Although the story sounded sincere, I had never heard a bad word against the sheriff. Daddy said the sheriff had the best rabbit-hunting dogs in the state. The two of them spent long winter days hunting.

Aunt Ada's head was pointed down, and I couldn't tell if she believed Bass or not. Finally she said, "The sheriff is a good man. We know him and he is not part of the gang that chased you. He's as set against vigilantes as the rest of the decent people around here."

"I guess when he let me out to pick tomatoes, I figured he was giving me a chance to run. Maybe he wanted me to get away and go far from here. To tell the truth, I didn't care if I was in jail. It didn't make much difference. I never had any special place to be. When the other convict hightailed it, it just seemed natural to run with him. I took my chance."

"Well, I guess we knew we weren't bringing Moses down from Yankee Hill," Aunt Ada said, examining my face. She smiled. I read in her smile a look I had never seen before.

I turned to Bass and said, "You can't stay here. When you are healed, you have to go." Aunt Ada started up the stairs.

Bass said, "If I spent my last moment in this basement, I would die knowing people sometimes care. A lady and a boy showed more courage and concern than I ever have or ever will. It sure didn't take courage to run out of the tomato field." Bass turned to me. "You're the hero, Austin."

His words stopped Aunt Ada. She leaned over the banister and said, "Everyone deserves dignity. Nobody here is a judge or a hero. Our only intent has been to try and right a wrong."

"Do you remember when you told me, 'We are good people'?" Bass said, moving to the bottom of the staircase. He touched the railing Aunt Ada held. "You were wrong. You are the best people."

"Are you scared, Bass?" I asked.

He turned to me and said, "By now I'm about numb. I've been in jail, been chased by some crazies..." He paused to watch Aunt Ada climb the final steps. Still facing the empty stairs, he continued, "That's the finest woman I've known. Wise. Pretty. Caring."

When he finished speaking, an awful silence took the room. My concentration was on discouraging him from wanting to stay in Morningside. "You'll be well enough soon to travel. Here's your map." I pulled a piece of school paper from my hip pocket. "Study it." Geography came easily to me. The map was a product of my own knowledge of the area and of time stolen from history class.

Bass took the map, then gave me his hand to shake. "Sorry," he said.

Whether Bass had given us the whole truth was not certain, yet I gained some peace from his confession. The sun was way in the west by now, and the lamp Aunt Ada had lit spread its light over the basement. The mystery of Sardine Man's truck remained, so I volunteered to investigate.

Approaching the black truck, I saw no sign of its driver. I searched both sides of the road, checking the heavy woods, then set my vision on the tight clump of trees nearest me —oaks, side by side with white pines, intertwined with prickly brier bushes, low-growing holly, and thriving high weeds. Out of the tangled brush the toe of a boot appeared, the leather torn near the toe. I stared at the boot until Sardine Man stepped forward and stood beside his truck.

"Your aunt is lucky to have such a fine patch of wild blackberries." He held in his hand a few wine-colored berries. "Should be fully ripe any day now." I took a step backward, biting into my lower lip. He opened the truck door, looking over the top of it as if he was studying the mountain beyond the woods. "This side of the hill is a mystery. Feel the breeze? It doesn't blow on the reverse side, where I live. And see the shadows? They fall a deeper purple, providing a safer place to hide."

His words sounded like a riddle, but I was too occupied in a prayer he would not ask me any questions to try and figure it out. I feared I might say the wrong thing and betray Bass, but I didn't have to worry long.

Sardine Man climbed into the truck and coaxed the engine to life. Out of the dust in the wake of the truck, I watched Sardine Man's arm extend from the open window, his firm hand in a gesture of good-bye.

I remembered the conversation in the graveyard and recalled Sardine Man's offer to help. I began to believe he was a guardian angel—not the spirit kind Miss Dixie often spoke about, but real.

—Chapter Fifteen—

Daddy's voice coming from somewhere out back drove me out of bed. I ran through the kitchen so fast Miss Dixie could not get a word out. But she trailed after me and yelled, "You'd better get in here and get some clothes on." Pulling my pajama top straight and hiking up the bottoms, I hurried to Daddy's side. He stood at the trunk of the car with a suitcase and a box beside him on the grass.

"Hey, Daddy," I said, stepping beside him to help carry the things into the house. Daddy slammed the trunk shut. "Where's Mama?" I asked.

"She's not ready to come back home yet, but she sends all her love," he said, hoisting the cardboard box onto his shoulder.

I circled my hand around the suitcase handle and said, "I'll take this in."

Daddy stepped before me and put his hand on mine.

"I'll take it," he said, walking to the truck, which was parked a few feet away. "I'm moving in with Nella for a while. She needs me to help get the tobacco up."

Every summer after the tomatoes had been harvested, Daddy helped his sister, Nella, cut her tobacco crop and haul it up in the rafters of her barn. He had never moved in with her before. After the box and suitcase were in the back of the truck, Daddy said, "Let's talk. Get in the truck." I climbed into the truck but left the door open. The cold plastic seats and the smell of stale cigarettes made me sad.

"Mama's not coming home," I said.

Daddy drummed a cigarette to the edge of the pack and pointed it toward me. "Want to light it?" Lighting Daddy's cigarettes was one of my Mama-forbidden treats. I took the Camel in my fingers. Daddy struck a match and lit the cigarette.

I handed the cigarette back to him. He took a deep drag. The smoke came out in a heavy stream. Daddy squinted to keep it out of his eyes. Leaning over the steering wheel, he said, "Your mama wants a little more time alone." His chest pressed against the steering wheel, and his hands hung over the top near the windshield. "I tried to get her back. I tried hard." His voice was soft but grew bolder when he added, "She'll be home. And I think as soon as she knows I'm giving her room by moving in with Nella, she'll be home even faster."

"How long are you going to stay at Nella's?"

"Just till your mama gets home and is comfortable again. Not long."

"So you don't know when Mama's coming home, and now you're going away again, too?"

Daddy had been looking at me, but he lowered his head at my question. He sucked on the cigarette, then looked at the back porch like he expected Mama to come walking through the screen door.

"Nobody will tell me why Mama went to Winston-Salem, and nobody talks about her anymore or knows when she's coming home," I said, propping myself side-saddle in the seat to make Daddy look at me. My knee was on the seat, and Daddy stared at the cowboys and horses on my pajama leg. He put his finger on a bucking horse and traced it with the tip of his finger.

"Maybe I needed to talk more to your mama," Daddy said.

"Did you have a fight?" I asked, following Daddy's hand as he traced around the cowboys on my knee.

"Not exactly." He sat back in the driver's seat like he just realized something. "It's hard to explain fully. Remember how hard it was for your mama to get over your grandpa's death?" I nodded, because I remembered Mama crying every day, in the kitchen, on the porch, at breakfast, at supper. "Well, it's like that. She's just having a hard time coming to terms."

I struggled to comprehend what Daddy's words meant.

"What does she have to come to terms with?"

"Things. Things you will learn later in life," he said, turning his face away as a sign he had said all he wanted to say. I studied him for a minute, but joined him in staring out the windshield rather than confronting him.

I often fussed with Miss Dixie and on occasion sassed Mama, but it never crossed my mind to argue with Daddy, so I slouched back against the cold seat. Although I was not going to argue for more details, I did ask, "What do you mean, you needed to talk more to Mama? Talk about what? About me?"

"No, not about you. You are the best thing for both of us. We talk about you all the time."

"Then what, Daddy? What did you need to talk about?"

"It's too hard to find words to tell you right now. It's something that happens sometimes to grown-ups, and it takes a while to get over it and kind of let the truth find its own way."

Daddy had always been quiet and peaceable, always giving in to Mama. On the other hand, Miss Dixie said Mama was sweet as a song, but could make a wasp cry. Mama used fast words and mean looks for weapons, but her outstanding armament was silence. When she was mad, she pouted. No words, no looks. Mama made everybody think they had disappeared.

"I feel I have to keep thinking about Mama or she'll never come back. She'll disappear like she never belonged with us."

"Your mama just needs time. She'll be home. Things'll get back to where they were," Daddy said. He grabbed my knee and squeezed until I squirmed off the seat and fell out the open door, laughing. That was Daddy's best weapon; he could tickle me until I laughed and rub his beard on Mama's neck until she did.

I emerged from my bedroom in my best pants and joined Miss Dixie in the kitchen. She had changed into Sunday clothes. Aunt Ada was going to drop her in West Asheville on our way to town to buy a sweater for Bass. Miss Dixie wanted to go to church on Sunday. She was leaving again, going back to her cousins', after being back home for only three days.

"Tie these apron strings so I don't get nothing on my good dress." Miss Dixie twirled round. To show I was angry with her for going away again so soon, I pulled the two white sashes as tight as I could and tied them in a knot. Miss Dixie turned her head and gave me a disgusted look.

I sat down at the table and continued to aggravate her. "If it weren't for coloreds, we wouldn't have to worry," I said. Miss Dixie kept to the business of packing the fresh-apple cake she was taking with her. "What makes you coloreds so mean?" The more Miss Dixie ignored me, the more I persisted. "Well, I guess you don't know why your kind is so mean." I braced for one of Miss Dixie's Jesus answers.

Without looking up, but with impatience in her voice,

Miss Dixie said, "We ain't no meaner than anybody else, when it come down to it. Shoot, I seen both colors mean as striped snakes."

"You better quit that cursing," I said.

I got the attention I was after. Miss Dixie turned and stepped toward me. She stared at me in disgust and said, "I ain't cursing. And don't you go telling I was, or, or..." She picked up a wooden spoon off the counter. "Or I'll wear you out with this spoon."

"Mama said saying *shoot* is the same as saying *shit*."

Miss Dixie threw down the spoon and grabbed my arm in a hearty pinch. I wrenched away, struggling up from the table and pulling a safe distance from her reach.

"Your mama ain't here right now, or you'd get your mouth washed out with soap," Miss Dixie said, struggling with the stubborn knots I had tied in the apron.

"Mama's never coming home," I said in my meanest tone, darting for the back door, slamming the screen, and holding it.

Miss Dixie said to my back, "Mister, you gonna get your comeuppance one of these days."

I plopped down in one of the rockers, rocking as fast as I could make the chair go. I said, "Miss Dixie was cursing again. I don't know what we are going to do with her. Shoot. Shoot. Shoot."

Miss Dixie began singing, her voice louder with every *shoot*. "...And I'll fly away, oh glory."

• • •

"What did Daddy do that made Mama go away?" I asked, once the car was on the four-lane headed for Asheville. Aunt Ada avoided looking at me, and I could tell she was not going to volunteer anything I did not ask.

"He didn't do anything," she said.

From the backseat Miss Dixie said, "The truth will set you free."

"Aunt Ada, it's not fair. Daddy said he can't find the words to tell me what's wrong, and you say he didn't do anything. What does it mean? You've always been honest with me, and I've never asked for too many favors, but I want to know."

Miss Dixie reached over the seat and handed over two peppermint drops. "Always good to have something sweet in your mouth when sour words are forming," she said, tossing a peppermint around in her mouth while she talked. I took the candies and put one on top of Aunt Ada's purse and popped the other into my mouth.

"When we get home. I'll tell you when we get back home," Aunt Ada said.

We got a navy sweater for Bass and a pair of corduroys. They were on the chair at the breakfast table when Aunt Ada opened the door to the basement and invited Bass to join us. A steaming mug of hot chocolate sat on the table before me. The cup was too hot to pick up, so I leaned into it and slurped the hot drink into my mouth, letting the sweet chocolate slosh over my tongue.

Aunt Ada took a deep breath and said, "I guess I'm going to have as hard a time telling you as your father did." Bass appeared at the kitchen door. "Close those drapes, Austin," Aunt Ada said, pointing to the windows over the dining table. I swooped them shut. She poured a cup of chocolate for Bass.

With cup in hand, Bass patted my shoulder before settling into a chair at the table. He said, "How are you, old man?" I was usually glad to see Bass, but I wanted Aunt Ada to finish telling me what happened to Mama.

Aunt Ada said, "Austin and I are trying to have a conversation about his mother and father." Bass raised his eyebrows. I gave him a disinterested frown. I did not want him involved in our conversation.

"Bass and I have discussed this," Aunt Ada said. My eyes tightened into a deeper frown. She continued where she had left off before Bass came into the room. "Your mother was upset. She began to have questions about her marriage."

"Upset? About what?"

Aunt Ada leaned against the kitchen counter. "I'll share what I know." She studied me over her cup. "But knowledge does not give you permission to judge. Knowing things only expands your ability to better understand."

"What are you talking about, Aunt Ada? I only want to know why Mama went away and when she will be home."

Bass butted in. "Sometimes a person loses perspective

and can't get a grip on what they're supposed to do. They start looking round to put the blame for their misery." He looked at me, and I guess my expression was blank. "Your mama started thinking your daddy was to blame for her problems. He got caught in the middle."

"What did she think Daddy did?" I asked.

The room was still. No one moved. Aunt Ada said, "She claimed he was in love with Velma Falls. But your mother has to come round to knowing the truth. And the truth is, she was wrong." Aunt Ada sounded like she was giving instructions for a math problem.

I was caught off guard. "Velma Falls? The woman who worked at the store when Grandpa was sick?" Aunt Ada stared at me. "You said she was a floozy. What could she have to do with Mama?"

"Maybe it was Velma's doing and had nothing to do with what your daddy wanted," Aunt Ada said.

"Why did Mama stop loving Daddy?"

"Love has nothing to do with it," Bass said, staring at Aunt Ada. She didn't return the look.

Getting up and pouring more chocolate in his cup, Bass said, "The things we make up in our minds have no reason."

"What about Mama? She's still gone." I felt tears welling up in the back of my eyes. Lowering my head, I said, "Will Mama come back?"

"Of course. This is her home," Aunt Ada said.

"Why didn't Mama come home when Daddy went after her?"

Aunt Ada breathed hard. "Because she wasn't ready to deal with things. Your mother has a lot on her mind. I'll call her soon and try to get her to come home."

"Daddy said she needed time," I said. Aunt Ada nodded, taking a sip from her cup. "Why did Mama get mad at you?"

"Because I told her the truth. She wasn't rational. I pray for her every night. She has to separate imagination from truth. I just want her to forget."

"How can she forget when she thinks she's been hurt?"

"She can." Aunt Ada carried her cup to the sink. "I know."

"Joe Winter?" I said. Aunt Ada turned from the sink with surprise in her eyes. "Miss Dixie told me."

"Bless Miss Dixie's heart. Joe Winter is my sad tale. But it wasn't all him, it was me, too. That was what I tried to get through to Louise. When these things happen, we have to step back and inspect ourselves."

Bass had been quiet. He fidgeted in his chair when I mentioned Joe Winter. Now he said, "Who's Joe Winter?" His question was muffled by the cup in front of his mouth. He held it as if the question came from someone else.

"That is history so old it's better forgotten." Aunt Ada ran water into the sink and spoke without turning.

"He was Aunt Ada's boyfriend," I said.

Aunt Ada switched on the radio. She said, "I'm excited about going to the dance in Hendersonville." Her eyes gently turned to Bass. "How do you like the new clothes?" On the radio, Dinah Shore was singing, "You call everybody darling...." Aunt Ada reached to adjust the volume.

"I don't know if it's a good idea, me going out in public," Bass said, handing the empty cup to Aunt Ada.

I rallied at the change in subjects. "We've got it all worked out. How to get you down the road without anybody seeing you. And Hendersonville is about thirty miles from here. Nobody will know you there." I sounded convincing. I wanted to go to the square dance, and if Bass refused to go, Aunt Ada might back out of taking me.

"It's the end-of-summer dance. A celebration. You have to go. It will be a celebration for the three of us." Aunt Ada sat down at the table, drying her hands on a dish towel. "You need to get out of that basement, and this will be like a good-bye for the three of us. You'll be gone next week. Remember?"

"If you think it's safe. I don't want any of us in danger," Bass said.

Aunt Ada and Bass talked on about the dance. I went to the bathroom and stayed there long enough to be believable. Instead of returning to the kitchen, I walked into the living room. I quit thinking about the trip to Hendersonville and went back to wondering about Daddy and Mama. I could not understand why Mama needed to rest.

I did not understand why Mama went away, when she always told me the only way to face a problem was to stand still.

Picking up one of Aunt Ada's cherished porcelain ladies, I felt like smashing it into the fireplace. My fingers encircled the tiny glass head, and I gazed at the painted face. I gently set the doll back in its place. I was tired and sat down cross-legged before the empty hearth. I sat there long after Bass had returned to the basement and Aunt Ada began her preparations for bed. Finally I made my way into the guest bedroom. After I was in bed, Aunt Ada came to the bedroom door. I pretended to be asleep. She closed the door, leaving it open a crack. I stared up into the darkness for a long time.

I jumped upright in bed when Aunt Ada rushed into the room. She covered my mouth with her hand and pressed a single finger to her own lips. My eyes asked what had happened. Aunt Ada leaned over me, whispering into my ear, "Someone's on the front porch." My every nerve tingled.

"Let's turn the lights on; maybe that'll scare them away," I whispered back.

"Listen," she said. I strained, trying to hear footsteps. "A car," she said. In the distance a motor started, and we could hear it moving farther away from our ears. We went from the bedroom into the living room. Watching out the window, we saw a car's headlights come out of the woods on the other side of the road and slowly move from under the shadows of tall trees. When it pulled into the moonlight, we could clearly see the bright yellow Ford.

"It's Bell Hitcher. That's his car," I said. We watched until it was out of sight. I could almost hear Bell Hitcher's warning that he always watched me. Aunt Ada and I hugged. We were both shaking.

—*Chapter Sixteen*—

I was not always around to observe Bass and Aunt Ada during their time together. What I learned came to me accidentally.

One afternoon after school, Aunt Ada sat on the porch, wearing a kimono she'd bought in Tokyo. I brushed her hair. "Do you ever regret we saved Bass?" I said, straining her blond-colored hair through the brush needles.

"Sometimes it's difficult to tell the hero from the fool. Only time will tell where we stand."

Since I stood in back of her and did not have to face her, I boldly asked, "Do you love Bass?"

Aunt Ada turned in the chair to search my face. Her indigo eyes reflected the shadows thrown by breezy leaves playing tag with the sun. I tried to look honest. Starting with slow, stubborn words, she said, "Love is like a flower.

If you plant it too shallow, the wind will carry away the topsoil, and roots can't establish."

"A flower?"

"A stick," Ada replied.

I refused to allow her to read any questions in my eyes, so I forced her face away from me by starting to brush her hair again.

Aunt Ada changed to light, quick sentences that rained down and left me stymied. "Well, how about a stick that's hot on one end and cold on the other?"

"I probably don't know what I'm talking about," she went on. "I have always seen people go after the wrong part of love. Like the stick, if you pick it up by the hot end it stings, so the only desire is for a cooling comfort, but you can't drop it. Then the stick grabs you, possesses you. You shake so hard your skull rattles, but you still can't let go of the stick." When Aunt Ada finished speaking, I stilled the hairbrush, trying to understand.

Aunt Ada sprang from the chair and advanced from the porch into her snapdragon patch. Before she spoke again, she faced me. Her expression and voice were pleasantly lit. "The greatest lesson to learn about love is that it can be still and gentle. That's so different from what I believed all this time. I always expected thunder and shooting stars." She smiled. Then she made a quick, uneasy nod as if she was ashamed of the conviction. She squatted and began weeding the flowers.

I watched her pull a tall weed, dangling it high. She raised her head. I tried to look like I understood. "That doesn't answer your question," she said. "I feel close to Bass. Real, true love takes a long time; time we'll never have." She flung the weed into the yard. "Anyway, you know I'm an old maid." She laughed. I was happy with her answer. It made me feel grown-up.

"Why don't we tell people about Bass? Get them to know what really happened to him. Get them to believe he's not a bad person."

Aunt Ada's eyes changed to a sad shade of blue. "People believe what they want to. It takes a special knowledge to believe in a person like Bass."

Thoughts paraded in my head. "Miss Dixie says the truth will set you free."

Aunt Ada sat down on the porch steps. She faced the pink afternoon sky. The hills grew dark green. "It takes most people a lifetime to learn what you and I know." I sidled down beside her. She lifted her arm and hugged me. It was in that instant that Aunt Ada confirmed she loved me.

Late the next afternoon, I entered Aunt Ada's house through the basement, expecting to find Bass at work on the model ship I had given him. The gray plastic parts were scattered on a worktable. I picked up a small flag, wiggling it into a groove at the stern of the ship. Voices, filtering from upstairs, distracted me.

The door at the top of the stairs was ajar. I walked deeper into the room, pausing at the foot of the staircase and staring up at the door. I could hear Aunt Ada talking in the kitchen above. Slowly I climbed, taking the last few steps in long, silent strides. Halting at the doorway to the kitchen, I realized Aunt Ada and Bass were in the breakfast room, just out of view. I leaned against the doorjamb and listened. Silence. Finally I was driven to crack the door wider and peep round the corner.

The room was painted with late afternoon sun, reflecting off the pale yellow walls and bouncing onto the polished oak-wood table. Bass and Aunt Ada sat at the table. He was in profile and played with a coffee cup. Aunt Ada's back was to me. The soft curves of her hair swirled down and floated over the cable pattern of her pale pink sweater. Her hand rested on the table, near Bass's cup. His shirt was unbuttoned.

In a voice light and summery, Aunt Ada said, "Your being here in my house has brought back feelings I thought I had no need for or could ever have again, even should I want them."

Bass released the cup and lifted his face. I had never known him to be so quiet. Last night he'd spoken of places he had been; he went on about Texas and Kentucky. Last week he'd talked of history, the Civil War; and before that he spoke of jail and justice. Talk, talk, talk. Words came easy to him. Subjects were never foreign. Yet, this moment, words stayed away. With eyes half-closed Bass tenderly eased his square-tipped fingers back and forth over Aunt Ada's thin wrist. This seemed a sort of settlement between them, a silent signal of protection.

A dead leaf, whirling up in a rush of wind, flew by the window and captured their attention. Still looking out the window, Aunt Ada said, "Winter's coming. The long, cold days ahead will fasten me to this hill. When that window is frosted, I'll remember the strength in your hand." She turned her head toward Bass but did not look up. "And I will wonder where you are, praying every time I pass this table or lie down in my bed that you've found a safe place."

Bass covered her hand with his. His eyes went wet-looking, and his gaze roamed over her hair and face. Aunt Ada said, "I'll miss you."

It seemed to me Bass held back words he wanted to say; his lips were tight. He leaned forward, wrapping his arm over Aunt Ada's shoulders, his head snuggled in her hair like he was hiding himself in the first leaves of spring.

With the subsiding sun a chill came. They did not talk anymore. The room became still and cold.

I pulled back safely beyond their view. I started to leave, but Bass's voice stopped me. "If I had one wish, it would be to live again and to find you."

In a voice softer than before, Aunt Ada said, "Along with the man I dragged off a mountain, I brought a life back for myself. Maybe we haven't the right to expect more."

Maybe it was half an hour I stood there, maybe a minute, alert to their affections. Their conversation scared me. I'd never witnessed such a final parting. I crept down the hall on the other side of the house. My feet moved sluggishly, as if I walked in high mud. I passed Aunt Ada's bedroom. The last of a somber sun lit the rumpled bed.

When I got to the front door, I slowly opened it, then eased it shut behind me, letting my fingers take the brunt of the closing. My feet stuck at the edge of the porch. I sat on the rough boards, pulling my knees to my chin and staring into the grass. Wandering into Aunt Ada's private moment excited but saddened me. I picked at a splinter sticking out of the pine floor. One thing I had learned: Miss Dixie was wrong; all the love had not left Aunt Ada's heart.

I swung off the porch and headed home. Before I reached the path that led through the woods to our house, Aunt Ada had started playing the piano, not a church hymn but a hymn of love. I had heard her play it before. The tune was misty and shadowy. I imagined Bass standing behind Aunt Ada, watching her fingers glide over the black-and-white keyboard. Then, in my mind, I saw them dancing, like in the movies. They were on a high hill with a perfect sky as background. Aunt Ada's skirt flirted with the breeze and Bass smiled so big all his teeth showed.

The next day was Friday and the dance I had waited all summer for. Just before final daylight faded, I walked, mostly skipping, to Aunt Ada's.

Aunt Ada backed the car out of the garage and pulled it onto the grass parallel to the basement door. The car faced the road. She drew the Chevy so near the house Bass could bolt from the door and get inside the car without being seen.

I opened the car door wide to block any view from the road. Bass stood in the open basement door, staring at me. I pulled the front seat forward so he could jump in back. Bass stood still. I motioned with my head toward the seat. He hunched over and hurled forward, brushing against my stomach. He struggled onto the floor between the front and back seats. Aunt Ada had spread a blanket on the floor-boards for cushioning. Once Bass was wedged into position, I threw a second blanket on top of him. Aunt Ada, on the driver's side of the car, helped me smooth the cover over him.

I climbed in the passenger's side. Aunt Ada's perfume made the car smell like Mama's rose garden. With her hand on the ignition key Aunt Ada looked at me, her eyes holding the same glow I had noted on that stormy night when we rescued Bass. I could not tell if she was excited or scared, but her look sent me a silent message that I was to be the sentinel. The last fraction of twilight struggled against a darkening sky, making it difficult to determine if the long shadows in the woods were cast by short trees or tall men. My heart quickened when I thought for an instant I saw Bell Hitcher standing square in the dense forest. A second look proved it was only a short pine.

Once we were on the two-lane to Hendersonville, Bass struggled up and sat in the middle of the backseat. I curled one leg under me, turning sideways so I faced him. His beard had grown in, and the new blue shirt Aunt Ada bought him reflected in his eyes, making them pools of sparkling blue. Framed against the rear window and in the dim moonlight, he looked like a movie star on the screen of a drive-in theater. Bass smiled. I wanted to ask if he was ready to make a serious attempt at running away, but his smile stopped me. Aunt Ada had said this was a fun time, and I feared a conversation about escape or capture would spoil the dance. I just smiled back.

Still smiling and inspecting Aunt Ada's hair, Bass craned to see her profile. He said, "You look especially pretty tonight, Miss Schoolteacher."

I wondered if Bass could see the smile coming to Aunt Ada's lips. The dim dashboard lights concealed any blush on her cheeks, but she gripped the steering wheel tighter. She did not answer. Her eyes stayed glued to the road, and the car's headlights fell on silent country curves.

When the streetlights of Hendersonville appeared in the distance, Aunt Ada turned the car from the main road onto one of the side streets. After parking several streets from the center of town, Aunt Ada stepped out of the car. Bass jumped out of the back and crooked his arm. She said, "Thank you." I did not know if she meant this for his support or for saying she was pretty. I walked a few steps behind, scouting every car we passed, hoping we were not recognized.

Hendersonville was lit up brighter than daytime. The

main street, blocked off by sawhorses, seemed wider without moving traffic. Bales of hay, piled two deep, formed spectator benches and freshened the night with the smell of new-mowed fields. A temporary stage supported a three-piece band. Above the stage, a flag waved in the night air. The bass and guitar players stood at the back of the platform, sparking a few notes and waiting for the crowd to gather force. On each end of the blocked street stood cider stands. The street filled with people, milling around, smiling over paper cups, and licking pink cotton candy off their fingers. I searched every face. And, like I had promised Bass, every face was that of a stranger.

Just as the three of us walked into the lighted crowd, the music started. I scooted onto a bale of hay. Bass pulled Aunt Ada into an area where people were paired up in a circle. The people, the music, the strangers seemed to give us permission to be normal, forget who we were and what secrets we held. A storm of fiddle music cut loose and freed every foot within earshot.

Aunt Ada's dress was the only red one. It reminded me of her snapdragon bed, which she took great pride in yet never picked. But yesterday, a vase had poured over with scarlet and yellow blooms, and Bass had sheepishly admitted picking the flowers. Aunt Ada did not protest the cut snapdragons.

A peekaboo moon spotted every dancer, and music, sweet as the cider dispensed at the concession stalls, anointed the blue night. My foot itched with every note from the band. When the square-dance tune was over, the fiddler played a slow love song.

Bass pulled Aunt Ada's head close to his shoulder. She rested her hand on his chest, where only weeks ago she had sewed life back into him.

I watched the faces of the spectators. Some smiled at the dancers. Others kept their eyes closed and swayed in time to the music. The sky was like a ribbon of steel, starless, and either the faint chill or the loud music scared off any fireflies.

For a moment I got caught up in the night and forgot who I was and who Bass was. Then I questioned why we were here, smiling, dancing. The excitement of saving a convict was over. Bass was well, and he proved it by the way he swung Aunt Ada around the dance floor. It was time for Bass to go.

I searched Bass's face. All traces of the convict were hidden; he seemed to be in a place no one had ever been. The music chased any dangers he had faced or was to face. Aunt Ada and I cared for him in our own special ways. Bass had proved he was no danger to us. How close to freedom was Bass, and how safe should Aunt Ada and I feel?

A girl with brown hair tied up in yellow ribbons glided down beside me. She kept glancing sideways at me. My heart beat a little faster. When the bandleader announced the next dance would be a cakewalk, she turned her full face to me and said, "Would you do the cakewalk with me? I sure would like to win a cake." Then, as if she felt a need to erase a selfish thought, she added, "Oh, you can have half of it if we win."

I nodded and was getting to my feet when hands clapped down hard on my shoulders. Before I could turn, lips were at my ear. "Baby boy." The smell of beer and tobacco came with the words. Lips were close to my ear, and I could feel the moisture of breathing. Before I could turn and face the voice, Bell Hitcher jumped over the bale of hay. He stood between me and the dancers. He raised his eyebrows and grinned. Then, just as quickly as he had found me, he vanished into the crowd.

Aunt Ada and Bass were at the cider stand. I started to run to them when the girl in the yellow ribbons said, "Didn't change your mind, did you?" I looked back to Aunt Ada, but she was in line for the dance by then. The girl took my hand, and we joined the other dancers.

For the moment, and for the next few minutes, my thoughts left Bell Hitcher and stayed on the girl with the ribbons.

My hands were sweaty, and I had to keep wiping them on my pants. The ribboned girl was silent while we walked around in a big circle. She did not even say a word all the times we stopped with the music. It seemed she just kept looking at the chocolate cake set out for the prize. When the final stop came and a man stepped up and announced the winner, the girl almost cried. She ran away without saying good-bye, and I walked over to Aunt Ada and Bass.

I watched the crowd break up, people climbing into cars and trucks, waving to us like we were their friends. I thought how normal we were and I wished every day could be like that moment. No one suspected who we were or what we did or what we were going to do, no one except Bell Hitcher. I kept searching the crowd for him.

My full fear of having encountered Bell Hitcher returned. Without letting Bass hear, I whispered to Aunt Ada that I had seen him. She looked at the few people near us and picked up her pace. Then she stopped. "We'll deal with that tomorrow," she said.

On the way back to the car, Bass teased me about my girlfriend. "Broke that little girl's heart; you didn't win a cake." I kept my face from him so he could not know I blushed.

Fearing more teasing from Bass, I started to talk about another subject. I asked, "Where will you go when you leave?"

Bass grabbed me at the shoulders and twirled me round, pulling my back against his chest. My head rested under his chin. "That way is Kalamazoo." He turned us both round and pointed east. "And over there is Timbuktu." Still holding me fast, he said, "Where would you go?"

"I don't know."

"Didn't you ever want to go somewhere so special you'd be a better person just for being there?" Bass asked.

I recalled Bass's philosophy of life. He had told me the

only words you ever need in this world are "perhaps" and "thank you." I answered, "Perhaps."

Bass released my shoulders but grabbed me round the chest. He was laughing hard, his chin burrowed into my neck. I started laughing, too, but my excitement was more from the tickling of Bass's beard. Thrashing hard to get loose, I accidentally pulled us to the ground. "Denmark," I screamed.

"Denmark?" Aunt Ada and Bass repeated in unison.

We all laughed. All thoughts of seeing Bell Hitcher fell out of my mind.

I lay on my back, recovering. The trees above me looked black-green, the lower branches a richer green like the perfect color I had tried to find in a kaleidoscope. Emerald green was the most beautiful color I had ever seen, but like all things of great beauty, it held an edge of sadness about it.

—Chapter Seventeen—

The next morning, I had been sitting on Aunt Ada's front porch well over half an hour before I heard what sounded like bathwater being drawn. Then I heard the key tumble in the front door. Aunt Ada pushed on the screen door with her elbow and stepped out on the front porch barefoot. She stretched back her head and gave an exaggerated yawn. "Good morning, good morning," she said, jumping off the porch, her kimono whooshing after her.

Aunt Ada noticed my attention was on the running water inside the house. "Bass is taking a bath," she said, kneeling to snap a dead flower from the flower bed.

"Let's talk about our plans for tonight. We need to figure out a way to get to the truck stop and make sure Bass knows how to get to Atlanta from there. I think I know a good route."

I was not sure Aunt Ada heard me, because she said,

"Did you have a good time at the square dance?"

"Yes, but once is enough for me." I answered her quickly, getting back to my original subject. "I've reworked the map so Bass can get his bearings better."

Aunt Ada came back on the porch. Opening the screen door and holding it open, she said, "Hungry?"

"I could stand a piece of pecan pie."

Aunt Ada laughed. "C'mon. You are getting more like me every day. I've always said if it's not half sugar, I can't take it on an empty stomach." She held the door for me. A fly buzzed into the house over our heads.

Bass came out of the bathroom, wearing a towel. "Good morning, Sleeping Beauty," he said to Aunt Ada. "And how's Romeo?" He was still kidding me about the girl in yellow ribbons at the dance.

Aunt Ada stepped close to me and whispered, "Got a secret. I called your mother. She'll be home on the afternoon train."

When I told Miss Dixie the good news, she said, "I've got cleaning to do. This place is gonna shine for your mama's homecoming. Got to wash the windows, scrub this kitchen floor, and bake a cake, too."

"An orange cake. She likes orange best," I said.

While Miss Dixie cleaned the house, I restaked Mama's red rosebush and pulled the dead flowers off the pink one. A few leaves were caught in the short fence that skirted the flower bed. With an old broom I swept away the leaves.

Miss Dixie, washing the inside of the living room windows, tapped on a windowpane. When I looked at her, she pointed to a section of the fence I had missed. Then she raised the window and yelled, "Maybe you should pick a few of the big roses for your mama's bedroom. But get the shears, 'cause them thorns will tear your hands up."

Cutting the flowers, I thought how every summer before this one had been remarkably identical. Even the scents of the previous summertimes repeated themselves in the same order. It was almost like a giant hand scooped up the smells of the season, stored them in a special jar, and sprinkled them down on us each year at the same time.

With one deep sniff I could tell the time of the month by whatever filled my nostrils. The strong odor of upturned soil fresh from Daddy's plowing started off the season. Further into June, when tomato plants bored through the brown earth, the smell of new leaves and honeysuckle circled up in the afternoon breezes. By midsummer the fragrance of Mama's roses floated over the fenced flower bed and perfumed the whole hill.

After I gathered the flowers and Miss Dixie put them in Mama's favorite vase, I helped Miss Dixie sort out rubber bands, used stamps cut from mail, S&H Green Stamps, and hairpins. These were some of the things Miss Dixie saved and kept in mason jars in the pantry. Mama called Miss Dixie a string saver and threw out the junk when she found it, so Miss Dixie had to get all the jars emptied before Mama got home.

The boxes under Miss Dixie's bed stored everything from Popsicle sticks, mostly contributed by me, to scraps of cloth sheared from discarded clothes. The solid-colored pieces were cut into squares, and the prints ended up in maple leaf or star shapes. There was also a box of toys I had outgrown or had broken. Around Christmastime, Miss Dixie fixed them up as best she could and gave them to children at her church.

"Miss Dixie, maybe we should just throw some of this stuff away," I said, growing tired of sticking saving stamps into a redemption book.

"No sir, Mister. I'm careful with what I throw away; no telling when I just might need something," Miss Dixie said, handing me a small photograph she pulled out of one of the jars. "Go put that in your mama's picture box." It was my first-grade school picture. I stared at the tiny image like it was somebody I used to know.

When I opened the cigar box to toss the photograph in with the assortment of other pictures, something shiny caught my attention. I raked the pictures to one side and found Mama's wedding ring. My fingers slid round the side of the box until they rested directly above the ring.

"You gonna help me finish this cleaning?" Miss Dixie's voice startled me. I grabbed the ring and put it in my pocket.

— Chapter Eighteen —

*R*ibbons of dusty light streamed through the tall windows of the freshly painted train station. The stale smell of a neglected building seeped from under the paint fumes. The scent matched the long oak benches bleached from too much time in the sun. It was 4:47 P.M. I watched the huge clock hands but blinked every time they changed, always missing the exact movement to the next minute. A hunched-over woman, heavy coat looped over her arm, paced under the clock; a well-traveled suitcase rested by the caged ticket teller; and more dust than air stirred from a corner pole fan.

"It might be cooler outside," Aunt Ada said. She tucked her flat straw-colored purse under her arm and started for the glossy green doors leading to the trains. Her high heels clicked on the concrete floor.

I searched the platform. A uniformed train worker was

the only other person in sight. The three tracks, covered by steep tin roofs, stretched from the station building into the hot sun and disappeared behind a bend surrounded by a clump of trees. We came to the platform where we assumed the train from Winston-Salem would stop. I brushed away a line of sweat running down my neck and pulled my collar into place, the way Mama always did. Buffing my shoes on the back of my pant legs, I straightened my shoulders to align with my hips. I tried to appear as if I had been braced against a board; Mama would be inspecting me.

"You'd never know it was September, with this heat," Aunt Ada said, using her purse for a fan and taking deep swipes at the stilled air. She wore a violet-colored dress that made her blue eyes look purple.

"Think Mama's still mad? At you, I mean," I said, more to pass time than for a real answer. Aunt Ada fanned faster, ignoring me. I was so happy Mama was coming home I didn't care if Aunt Ada talked or not. Daddy had willed Mama back. She had had her time away, alone; now she could come back and let us all be happy, like before. Mama would be home today, Bass would be gone tonight, and maybe Daddy would come back home from Nella's by Sunday. There would be no more danger, and the peace we knew before this summer would return to Morningside.

"Do you think Mama wants to see Daddy before we go home?" I asked, still trying to stir conversation. Aunt Ada had ambled down the platform. She stopped to run the toe of her shoe down a crack in the cement. "I mean, will

Mama want to talk to Daddy and find out when he is coming back home?"

Aunt Ada walked to me but continued to stare at the platform floor. "I'm not even going to give her an option. She needs to get settled. Your mother sounded fine on the phone, but she has such a hard time accepting changes. She would even like you to stay a boy forever. We're going to take her home so she can settle in before having to think about anything else."

Nothing could spoil Mama's homecoming, not even Aunt Ada's insinuation that Mama's return would not bring us total happiness. With Mama home, my time would be spent being near her, trying to guess what she wanted done and having it finished before she got round to asking. We would plant yellow chrysanthemums in the flower boxes on the store windows. Mama always changed the boxes to mums this time of year. And I would find small pumpkins, the ones she liked, to put in with the flowers.

She would work at the store, like before, and I would go there after school to load the shelves. She would let the John twins go. Daddy had hired them to tend the store; most times the twins worked on Saturdays, which relieved me and Miss Dixie from having to keep the store. But maybe the John twins would stay on for Saturday work, and Mama could stay home on weekends and make lemon pies. One thing for sure, Velma Falls would not work in the store. She would not be round to make Mama leave again.

And Bass. What would Mama say? She would be scared,

just like Miss Dixie. But Bass would be gone tonight. Aunt Ada and I would take him to the truck stop. He would escape and would be in Atlanta before me and Mama awoke safe in our own beds on Sunday morning. Mama need never know. Even should Miss Dixie tell her, it would be after Bass had become a small history for me and Aunt Ada.

I was excited and a little nervous. Every time a bell sounded or cars shunted on far tracks my stomach jumped. The click, click of Aunt Ada's shoes sounded like matches being struck. I jumped when lights blinked from red to green and summoned a rush of train workers. One man carried wooden steps and hobbled down the track away from us, and he kept checking his watch, peering deep down the track. We heard the train before it came into view. A single black engine pulled round the bend and crawled toward us. The brakes wheezed, and the train screeched to a halt. Only the engine and the first of six cars came to rest in the shade of the terminal roof. Aunt Ada and I hurried toward the man with the steps, and I strained to see Mama's face pressed against one of the train windows.

When a man in a blue uniform waved the passengers down the steps, they bounded off the train and rushed into the station building. Aunt Ada and I scooted back to let them pass. Suddenly, Mama appeared in the door, taking the hand of the train porter and pausing on the last step to search for us.

We saw her, but she yelled, "Here I am, over here."

Mama looked beautiful. She wore a dark red dress with a sparkling pin on one shoulder. Running to us, her hair bounced like angel wings, and she smelled like summer flowers. No tears, just smiles and smiles. Mama was home. An extended hug told her how much I needed her. "I missed you," she said close to my ear.

Aunt Ada continued to fan herself. "Louise, I've never seen you looking so wonderful," she said, giving Mama a faint kiss on the cheek. They did not hug.

"Maybe heartache agrees with me," Mama said.

We lugged Mama's suitcases to Aunt Ada's car. She said they were heavy because she had loaded them down with presents for me. With Mama and Aunt Ada in the front seat of the car, I sat on the edge of the backseat, hovering over every word they said.

"How's Miss Dixie doing?" Mama asked.

"Same as ever," I said. "Cursing, dipping snuff, and spitting in the sink."

"Austin, you are a terror. I bet you've run that poor woman crazy," Mama said, smiling. Aunt Ada laughed. I made them happy. It was just like old times.

Mama turned in her seat to face me. She said, "Well, it looks like Miss Dixie had time to cook a little. You've filled out some."

"I'm eleven now, Mama."

"And here's your birthday present." She handed me a department store box. I pulled out a brown sweater with a circle of yellow reindeer running around the middle. I went on about the sweater for a long time, but the real present was Mama's coming home. When we were about halfway home and the conversation calmed down, Mama pulled something big and red from a huge shopping bag. She slid it over the seat to me. I must have looked surprised, because she said, "It's not a doll, it's a clown."

The clown was made in one piece and stuffed with cotton. It had squared-off arms and legs and a plastic painted face, and except for the fuzzy yellow pom-poms down its front and on top of its cap, the clown was shiny red satin. "I wanted you to have a keepsake. In a year or so the sweater will be outgrown"—she reached over the seat and caressed the clown—"but you can have this forever." I kept staring at the doll, realizing Aunt Ada might be right. Mama wanted me to stay her little boy.

Later that day, when we sat on the back porch, I kept my eyes on Mama. Even in the housedress she'd traded her red dress for, swatting at afternoon insects, she remained beautiful. She fluttered out her hair, stretched back her neck, straightened, then settled her attention on me. The porch swing rocked to her gently paddling feet. "School going all right?" she asked.

"I ride with Aunt Ada. Haven't had to take the bus yet. Oh, and I got a man for a teacher," I said.

Miss Dixie tromped across the kitchen and onto the porch. The screen door slapped behind her. "Lemonade," she said, steadying a tall pitcher and three glasses on the wicker table next to me. Chunks of lemon swam among the ice cubes. She poured from the side of the pitcher, letting the ice splash into the glasses. She handed the first glass to Mama. "Sure good to have you home," she said.

"I guess it's good to be back." Mama looked over the yard. Her eyes stopped on the tomato patch. I figured Aunt Ada had told her about the convicts and about Grandpa's house burning. She said, "What a foolish thing to do, bringing convicts out here."

"I told him you'd have a fit," Miss Dixie said, shaking her head and slurping her drink.

I tried to change the subject. "Daddy said we made a lot of money on the tomatoes."

Mama did not seem to hear. She said, "Poor Papa. Everything that remained of him gone to smoke."

We sat silent for a while. Finally, I said, "Mama, how do you know what to be afraid of?"

She stared at me. "Afraid? Are you afraid?" she asked.

Miss Dixie said, "Be afraid of everything. Every beast, every bug, every man, and God. You'd better be afraid of God."

"Now, Miss Dixie. I wouldn't go that far," Mama said. Miss Dixie was sucking on an ice cube and could not answer back.

"I'm afraid of snakes, and Indians, and things I can't see in the dark, and things I can't understand," I said.

Miss Dixie swallowed hard and said, "Convicts? You ain't scared of convicts?" She raised her eyebrows and stared at me. I could tell she was about to start talking about Bass and tell Mama everything she knew about me and Aunt Ada hiding him.

Mama said, "I guess what frightens me most is myself. I'm scared I'll wear the wrong dress, smile at the wrong time, say the wrong words, or hurt somebody's feelings without meaning to. Most of all, I fear losing the things I love most."

I thought Mama's words were strange. But before I could question them, Miss Dixie said, "Uhm. That ain't the same scared. Shaking scared, what he means." Miss Dixie pointed to me. "The Bible says a man shortens his life by foolish acts, and not fearing the bunch of fools round here could sure cut you short."

Mama stepped off the porch. She surveyed the spent vegetable garden. I jumped up to follow her, but when I reached her side, she said, "I need to be alone for a while."

I watched her walk away from me, cross the tomato field, and lean against a shaggy oak. Her back was to me. She stared at the charred ruins of Grandpa's house.

About that time, Aunt Ada, wading through high weeds, ambled toward me. Her arms were folded across her chest, and a baggy brown sweater hung down her sides. I met her at the center of Mama's summer garden. We both watched Mama a field away from us.

To break the silence I said, "A few onions are still growing over there." I lifted a finger toward some tall green stems.

"Reckon they'd be any good?" Aunt Ada asked.

I reached and yanked at the stems. My grip was not far enough down the plant. It broke. I bent over and grabbed the willowy greens near the ground. A giant onion plopped up. I held it out for inspection. "Too big," she said, smiling. "I bet your mother missed the garden. In Winston-Salem all they have are tomatoes, growing in with the flowers."

The golden afternoon sun dipped behind trees; shadows crept over the garden. "You're right, Mama's changed," I said.

"Let's just be glad she's back home with us." The toe of Aunt Ada's shoe dug a hole in the dried dirt. "Everything's gone to seed," she said.

"I didn't tell Mama about Shadow getting killed because I don't want her to be sad." I jerked up my shoulders, ramming my hands deep into the pockets of my everyday corduroys. I kept my face away from Aunt Ada. I stared at the weeds, trying to focus on the ones close to the ground, the ones that survived the cold nights.

"You are so lucky. Eleven years old and an almost perfect life. If we don't count the time you wrecked the bicycle and had six stitches to sew up your knee. But you healed up fine, and other than that fateful time you are one lucky guy." Aunt Ada made no attempt to hide her cheer-

me-up speech. She breathed in real hard like she was trying to suck the gold out of the sun. Her hands dropped and
fumbled for the pockets in her sweater.

"Shadow getting killed was the worst thing that ever
happened," I said.

Aunt Ada untwisted her hands out of the sweater
pockets and wrapped an arm round my shoulders. She
brushed my hair back. "Abou Ben Adhem (may his tribe
increase!)/Awoke one night from a deep dream of
peace,/And saw, within the moonlight in his room,/An
angel, writing in a book of gold."

Aunt Ada had taught me the poem when I was six or
seven. She said it was a spirit lifter. Small shadows cast by
twinkling leaves roamed Aunt Ada's cheeks. When she finished the poem, I asked, "Why do you always skip the part
about the lily?"

"It's too sad."

"I think it's the prettiest part of the poem."

A seriousness poured over her face. "Every beautiful
thing in this world is temporary. The loveliness of a lily in
bloom will end. That's why it make me sad. Can you understand what I mean?"

"I think I can. It's like Bass having to leave, but wanting
to stay with you." I paused and looked across the garden at
Mama. She still leaned against the tree, but the daylight was
fading and her image was losing detail; soon she would be
only a silhouette. "It's like Mama coming home, but not
being like she used to be."

Aunt Ada raised her head and stared at the sunset.

I began, "Abou Ben Adhem (may his tribe increase!)/Awoke one night from a deep dream of peace,/And saw, within the moonlight in his room"—Aunt Ada joined me—"Making it rich, and like a lily in bloom,/An angel, writing in a book of gold."

—Chapter Nineteen—

*B*efore unlatching Aunt Ada's basement door, I scanned the road and the woods' edge, taking the same precautions I had taken for the past six weeks. The large grove of trees near the house was a clump of black against the dark gray sky. With the nip of fall in the air, most of the crickets had died off. A few remained, but their noise was muted and cheerless.

I stood outside the basement longer than usual. Finally, with no danger in sight, I pushed open the door and jumped inside. My sudden entrance caught Aunt Ada and Bass in the middle of a long kiss. Their embrace did not surprise me as much as I surprised them. They pulled apart and Bass picked up a blue sweater and pulled it over his head. He wedged his shirtsleeve between the tips of his fingers and palm, working each arm into the sweater. I could smell the new wool. Aunt Ada wore a gray skirt and blouse.

She had pulled back her hair and pinned it. Their clothes made them look serious and almost scared me.

No words were spoken. Our careful plans had been rehearsed too often to need repeating, and each of us knew our mission. Bass would huddle undercover in the backseat while Aunt Ada drove west beyond Canton until we came to a truck stop somewhere this side of Maggie Valley. Trucks carrying cargo from the Champion paper mills would be a good bet for a hitchhiker. Bass could hop a ride across the Smokies into Tennessee, hitchhike south to Chattanooga and from there into Georgia. He could be lost in Atlanta by this time tomorrow.

I got lonely seeing Aunt Ada and Bass walk away from each other. Some part of me wanted Bass to stay, to stay and grow old with Aunt Ada. *Let us all be happy and safe,* I added to a quick silent prayer. But Bass had to go. He could not stay, now that Mama was back. If she learned of Bass, she would not be as easily evaded or tolerant as Miss Dixie had been. But even more threatening than Mama learning about Bass was that Bell Hitcher might find out.

I looked to Aunt Ada, to recover the courage I'd begun to lack. She went about the room the same way I had observed her at school: crisp and official, her steps purposely spaced, daring any question of her authority. The familiar sound from her high heels brought the only comfort.

Bass reached to the small lamp, killing the light. Total darkness surrounded us. Allowing a few seconds for our eyes to adjust, I opened the door. The three of us silently and quickly moved to the car. We had no shadows; the moon was buried in thick, stationary clouds. Lack of any light forced us to rely on sounds. The only noises we heard came from falling acorns, shifting leaves, and other unexplained disturbances that I attributed to passing cats, raccoons, and Indian spirits. There was not a single sound of harm; it reminded me of Christmas Eve.

Once inside the garage, Bass crawled beneath the blanket spread over the backseat. I took my place beside Aunt Ada, who already had the car's motor running.

The Chevrolet cleared the garage, and we backed past the house to the road. I wanted to ask Aunt Ada why she had not turned the car round and pulled it in the yard next to the basement door, the way she had when we took Bass to the square dance in Hendersonville, but it turned out that backing out was the best alternative.

Just as the car cleared the front of the house and we could see the woods on the other side of the front yard, our faces lit up in a yellow glow. The light came out of the woods about fifty feet from us. It was bright and unsteady. Leaning toward Aunt Ada's side of the car and squinting, I could see the light came from three torches. Because I was low in the seat I couldn't see who held the torches.

Aunt Ada's hands tightened on the steering wheel. I grabbed onto the seat with both hands. I heard my heart racing. "Get down," Aunt Ada said to me.

"What's wrong?" Bass's voice came as a muffled plea.

"Don't move," Aunt Ada whispered. She maneuvered the gear lever into park, leaving the car idling. Her hand fumbled with the door handle until the door gave and she kicked it open with her foot. She stepped out into the spotlight.

I struggled against the tight corner of the floorboard, trying to stay out of the wavery light that fell through the opened door. My head pushed against the dashboard, and I drew my legs flush against my chest. Aunt Ada snapped the car door shut. For a moment she stood before the door with her back to the window, then she moved from the car and toward the light. Her shadow disappeared. At the sound of voices, I listened hard but could hear only mumbles.

Bass worked himself up so he could see me through the crack between the two seats. I wanted to hate him for getting us into this night, but thoughts of Aunt Ada facing the light alone blocked out all others. Then guilt climbed into my every nerve. It was my fault. If I had left Bass on Yankee Hill, Aunt Ada and I would be safe. I wanted to jump out of the car and explain to the nameless torches that it was me to blame, not Aunt Ada.

Bass stuck his finger through the seats to get my attention. He whispered, "Unlatch the door, easy, then reach up and push the car out of gear. It'll roll down the hill out of the light. I'll work my way to your side of the car and jump out the passenger door when we are out of the light." Only a sliver of Bass's face was visible through the crack. He must have seen my worry at his suggestion, because it seemed a long pause before he said, "It's a chance, anyway."

I reached behind me and over my head and lifted up the cold metal handle, being careful not to push the door open. Then I slid over the rough flooring to the driver's side. Bass made the same journey to the passenger's side of the back-seat floor. Rolling onto my side, I positioned my arm to yank the gear.

With a rough tug I jerked the gear lever. In my attempt to release the gear quickly I accidentally landed an elbow on the gas pedal, zooming the sedan toward the garage. The passenger door flew open. At what seemed the same instant, a shotgun blast hit the car. Glass flew onto the front seat and sprinkled my head and arms. I closed my eyes. The car banged against what I assumed to be the front of the garage. I opened my eyes to glimpse Bass's shoes and cor-duroy pants slithering out of the car door.

Then came shouts, muted at first but growing louder and clearer. I looked up to see the light I had seen in the front yard now brightening up the dark backyard. I hugged the floorboard, but I could tell by the way the interior of the car glowed that the torches were still on the other side of the yard, away from the car. I heard another shout and curled myself tighter and pressed my head hard against my hands, grinding them into the chips of glass scattered over the floor.

—Chapter Twenty—

*T*he sounds and motions outside the car sped up, and yet my reactions seemed to be in slow motion. I closed my eyes and shook my head, shaking the glass splinters from the broken window out of my hair. Screams and shouts echoed around the car, but none of it made any sense. I looked up at the car windows. One side was a blazing yellow, the other cold black.

"Out of there," a voice yelled from the yellow side of the car. "Get out of that car."

I pushed the bigger pieces of glass aside, ignoring the sting from the jagged edges slicing into my fingers. Steadily pulling against the floorboards, I wormed my way to the open door from which Bass had escaped.

I slung my legs out the door and landed my feet on the ground. Slowly I pulled upright, sitting on the edge of the car's floorboard, but still shy of the lit side of the car.

My hands began to hurt, and a full cut on my thumb leaked blood into my palm. I had started to nurse my wounds when Sardine Man's truck swung into the driveway and stopped near the front of the house. The truck's headlights flooded the driveway and spotlighted the back of Aunt Ada's car. Sardine Man jumped from the truck and yelled to the backyard, "Don't shoot. It's me, Otis Stiller." He hurried to my side. Bass crouched down in the dark woods beside the garage and huddled against the building.

Sardine Man saw Bass, but yelled to the torches, "It's only the boy." He glanced at Bass and motioned with his hand for Bass to move into the woods. I pointed to the woods and then used my thumb to direct him to the road. I knew once he was hidden in the thick woods, he could work his way up the side of the driveway without being spotted.

Bass looked at me. I nodded a confirmation.

Sardine Man again yelled over the top of the car to the torchlight, "There's nobody here but the boy." Bass disappeared into the woods.

"Damn, I thought we had him." A voice came from the light. "Well, get that baby boy out here where I can see him." I could tell by the growing brightness that Bell had taken a few steps toward the car.

Rising with my back to the light, I watched my shadow grow full-size. By standing up and letting Bell see me, I had stopped his coming any closer to the car. I stubbornly turned round, as if a steady hand pushed at my back. My legs were wobbly, but Sardine Man braced my arm to steady me. Shielding my eyes, I looked over the car. Aunt Ada stood in the center of the yard, and three torches lit up the faces of the three Hitchers.

A noise at the front of the house made Sardine Man and me turn. Footsteps were running out of the darkness toward us. At first I thought it might be Bass, but when I squinted hard I made out Mama and Miss Dixie. The sound of a trigger being cocked made me look at the Hitchers. Bell had speared his torch into the ground and had his rifle wedged into his shoulder.

Just as Mama and Miss Dixie rounded the corner of the house and were in Bell's gun sight, a gunshot rang out. Sardine Man ducked behind the car and jerked me down with him.

I heard Miss Dixie yell, "Stop it, stop it. Why are you shooting at decent people?" Sardine Man blocked my view, but her voice seemed to come from the ground.

Aunt Ada screamed, "Look what you've done!" Sardine Man let go of me and rushed out into the torchlight.

I ran my hand along the cold metal until I reached the trunk of the car. From there I could see the yard. Miss Dixie squatted down on the grass, but she turned her head and saw me. She stood up and shouted, "It's only the boy. Don't shoot again."

She regained her full height and hurried to the back of the car, standing in the full beam of the truck's headlights. I moved toward her. Blood covered the front of her apron and tear tracks lined her face. I thought she was shot. She beckoned me to her. I could not resist the silent pleading. She grabbed me and pulled me into her arms in a strong hug. My head fell onto her shoulder, forcing me to look at the backyard.

Sardine Man hovered over Mama, who was flat on the grass. Aunt Ada knelt beside her and lifted Mama's head into her lap. I struggled for my freedom, but Miss Dixie tightened her embrace.

Sardine Man stood and addressed Mr. Hitcher. "This is serious. I got these boys out of trouble once before, but this is a real different situation." The torches backed up, taking the better part of the light with them. "You'd better get out of here."

The Hitchers stumbled backward, carrying away most of the light, leaving only the torch that Bell Hitcher had staked in the ground. In a few minutes we heard a distant car motor crank and roar away from our hearing.

"She is all right. Took a hit in the shoulder, but mostly knocked the wind out of her," Sardine Man said, coming toward me and Miss Dixie. "I'll take care of her. You take care of your business." He tossed Miss Dixie the truck keys. We both stared at the dark backyard. "She's fine," he reassured us.

Sardine Man and Aunt Ada spoke in low voices about their plans for Mama. I said, "Come on, Miss Dixie, we've got to help Bass."

Miss Dixie stared at me. I took her hand and started

toward the truck, trying to pull her with me. She stalled like a planted post.

"It ain't right," she said.

"You won't help?" I asked.

Miss Dixie stepped back. The keys jingled out of her hand and fell into the grass. Snatching them up, I started toward the truck, but stopped in front of the full beam of the headlights. Without facing Miss Dixie I said, "Be careful of the things you throw away."

I remained still until Miss Dixie was by my side. Turning toward her, I presented the keys in my open palm.

Miss Dixie climbed into the truck while I looked in the truck bed, but Bass was not there. Miss Dixie motioned with her head toward the pines beside the truck. The trees moved. Bass crawled out at my feet and said, "Turn off the headlights." Miss Dixie leaned forward in the driver's seat to search for the light switch. When she cut off the lights, the night blinded us. Miss Dixie waited to start the engine until we felt the truck rock a little and we knew Bass was settled in the back.

"Let's go the back way, Miss Dixie. I'll show you." I would take us the way Daddy went to buy baseball-pool tickets, way off the highway.

The old truck was cranky and bounced us around like we were intruders. I said, "Miss Dixie, Aunt Ada will be proud she taught you to drive."

"Now you gotta hush. I can't concentrate on the road and talk, too."

I wondered why Miss Dixie was not protesting the journey. But I figured she was probably as shocked as I, having seen Mama down and looking lifeless.

After a few miles and a good distance from Morningside, Bass tapped on the window. We stopped and he climbed into the truck and took the wheel. I navigated us across Hooker's Gap and Pigeon Valley to a dark spot where we got on the Canton highway. We skirted the town and headed toward Maggie Valley.

I had been to Maggie Valley and beyond several times but had never noticed the truck stop. It turned out to be just like I had pictured it in my mind. A jukebox bellowed out of the tiny building, a red-and-blue neon sign swung in the picture window of the café, and a silver truck parked near the window picked up the light.

Bass pulled the truck way over to the dark side of the building and turned off the headlights, but he left the engine running. Miss Dixie slid under the steering wheel when Bass left it and walked to my side of the pickup.

He leaned in the window. I could feel his warmth. "Tell Ada, I…" He lowered his head without finishing.

I ended the sentence. "That you'll see her in Kalamazoo."

He lifted his face, and it brightened. He stuck his hand inside the truck and put it on my head like Daddy always did. "And I'll see *you* in Timbuktu."

From my shirt pocket I took the picture of Aunt Ada

I had prepared. I had taken the snapshot of her and Joe Winter and cut away all evidence of the man in the picture. The result was a happy picture of Aunt Ada with a pair of arms wrapped round her waist. I pushed the picture into Bass's hand. He glanced at it and curled his lips into the same toothy smile he gave me the first time I saw him in the tomato field.

"Bye," I said.

Bass backed away from the truck, still smiling.

—Chapter Twenty-One—

*F*or a moment I could not tell if sleep had ended or I still dreamed. I pulled the pillow round my head, but the cough of Sardine Man's truck repeated in my ears. The pillow slipped from my grasp, tumbled off the bed, and plopped on the hardwood floor. The dull sound startled my eyes open. I pushed up from the bed and stared out the window at a misty morning.

The hastily abandoned clothes from the previous night lay in a rumpled pile by the door. I picked up the shirt and stabbed an arm into a sleeve. Working my way through the wrinkles, I tugged until the shirt was on. Then I ironed at it with my hand.

I cracked the bedroom door and listened for signs of life in the other rooms. Only the soft sound of Miss Dixie's little snores disturbed the silence. I tiptoed down the hall, pausing at the kitchen door to ensure I had not roused Miss

Dixie. Outside, the fall weather bit into my arms and made me feel naked. I could tell the sun had risen, but it hid in dense fog. Away from the trees, a skim of frost covered the open ground; the leaves would turn color fast now.

I rode my bike through the fog to the shack on the Hitcher property. When I neared the building, low voices filtered from the open door and gave me reason to stop short of my destination. I pushed the bike backward, letting the heavy mist provide a curtain between me and the shack. I squinted to see Mr. Hitcher exit, followed closely by Sardine Man. Mr. Hitcher ducked to miss the top of the short door frame, but Sardine Man cleared it easily. Their voices were sharper now.

"Well, you've probably got the best idea. I'll get the boys packing," Mr. Hitcher said. Sardine Man settled on a high black stump. "We'll start out before nightfall. I'll have them in Florida tomorrow, and they'll be in the navy as soon as they can get registered."

Sardine Man leaned back and said, "Maybe the navy will season them."

Mr. Hitcher breathed hard and started off into the fog, then paused and said, "If that schoolteacher wasn't so secretive, my boys wouldn't have had cause to be over at her place and nobody would have got hurt."

"Everybody's got a right to their own business," Sardine Man said.

Mr. Hitcher walked into the fog, away from the shack. His departure gave me the chance to move closer to

Sardine Man. A pipe rested in his hand. He watched two kittens play beside his worn boots. Finally, when he acknowledged me, I raised my eyebrows in a question before turning to watch a fat orange cat preoccupied with a serious bath.

"We took your mama to the hospital, your aunt and I."

"That's what Miss Dixie thought," I said.

"She's fine. The doctor said just a graze."

"We're going to see her today."

Sardine Man asked, "Did you do it?" I leaned on my bicycle and nodded. He strained to see through the fog. "Where's my truck?"

I pointed. "Down by the fork of the road. We left it there last night, too scared to bring it any closer."

"You took the man to Canton?"

"We took him to the destination we planned." I hesitated. With a deeper voice I said, "No need talking about things we've taken care of. What you don't know won't get you in trouble. I understand what we did was at cross-purposes to the Hitchers."

A black-and-white cat showed up, walked to my leg, and placed its head flat against me. I watched it over the handlebars of the bike.

Sardine Man disappeared into the dark interior of the shack. He returned with an oblong tin, rolled off the top, and put it down for the cat.

"You buy the sardines for the cats," I said. He did not answer. Instead he poked the pipe between his lips and lit it. The fog began to rise like smoke clearing from an enormous battle. I thought for a moment Sardine Man controlled the mist with his pipe. It seemed he was sucking away the haze into the pipe and exhaling a pure, clear morning.

I mounted my bike, but paused for one last question. "How did the Hitchers know we were moving Bass last night?"

"Bell had his eye on you and your aunt. I think he just made a guess that something was up."

On the way home, I lifted my feet from the bike pedals and coasted in a soft autumn wind that scooted under the remaining haze and nudged the ground fog up and away from the land. Slowly, light spread over the valley, and more light gave shape to hills. A full morning sun sparkled on the remaining frost. The views were familiar and real, and I'd never been so happy to be in Morningside.

I halted the bike in respect for a flock of geese flying overhead. Watching the birds, I took the piece of Teaberry gum from my pocket. Over the past six weeks the gum had become brittle. I chewed hard on it until it softened. I smoothed out the wrapper and was about to stuff it into my shirt pocket. The rainy-day box had been emptied of everything but the blue jay's feather, and I planned to give that to Aunt Ada when she had one of her blue days. Wadding up the pink gum wrapper, I flung it far into the weeds beside the road. Somehow I was beginning to figure out that happiness comes at odd times and in strange ways, and that real treasures could not be stored in boxes.

I was thinking all the way to the hospital about how I could tell Mama I was sorry. But when I saw her, all the rehearsed words left me. She wore a green robe that seemed fuller on one side. Standing at the window that faced the little park across the street, she said, "They have ginger ale here, if you want one." She turned to face me. Heavy white bandages dressed her shoulder, and her arm was in a sling. A lump came to my throat.

"Invincible," she said. I guess I looked startled, because she added, "Not as bad as it appears."

"I probably didn't do the right thing, Mama. I mean about the convict."

"*Shhh.*" Mama moved toward me.

"It wasn't Aunt Ada's fault. I talked her into helping me."

Mama sat down on the small white bed and signaled me to join her. Daddy, who had been close behind me, stayed by the door to the room. Mama said, "Miss Dixie told me all about it, last night." I sat down on the bed, sucking in my lower lip and staring at the wall.

"Aunt Ada says our hearts don't always follow the rules," I said, leaning toward Mama's good shoulder.

"Well, that sounds like Ada," Mama said, smoothing out the shoulder of the brown birthday sweater I had worn to please her.

I propped up on one hip so I could get my hand into my pants pocket. When I had my fingers round Mama's wedding ring, I slipped it out of my pocket and put it in the palm of her hand. Without looking at the ring, Mama said, "Do you think it will still fit?"

Leaning against the doorjamb with his head lowered and his hands clasped before him, Daddy said, "It'll fit just fine."

When I started down the hospital steps, Miss Dixie yelled out of the car window, "Is your mama all right?"

"She says she can come home on Tuesday." I walked to the car and propped myself against the front door. "Where's Aunt Ada?"

Miss Dixie's hand poked out of the car window, a strong, wide hand with one badly crooked finger: the result of the slip at the sewing machine. She pointed to the park across the street, the one Mama had been staring at from her window.

A word popped into my head. A word I'd never said but had read in a book. "Redoubtable."

I stared at Miss Dixie. She said, "What?"

"Redoubtable. That's you, Miss Dixie. *Redoubtable.* That's your word."

Miss Dixie curled her hand into a fist. "Mister, don't start in that mess with them words."

"It's a good word," I said, jumping round, proud I finally had a word for Miss Dixie.

I bounded up the six rock steps to the park and ran to Aunt Ada. She sat in one of the wide-boarded swing seats, softly rocking back and forth. The thick chains holding the swings shimmered in the setting sun.

"Mama's okay," I said.

Aunt Ada left the swing and walked to a lone oak tree at the crest of the hill. I trailed after her. "Do you think we will ever see Bass again?"

Moving forward, Aunt Ada stepped free of the tree's shadow. She stood in front of me and faced the sunset, focusing on the mountains and sky. "I don't know," she said, "but that's a splendid thought."

I stepped beside her and let the bloodred sunset wash over me. "Splendid," I repeated. It was the first time I ever heard anyone use that word.